THE DAY HE LET GO

HAWTHORNE HARBOR SECOND CHANCE
ROMANCE BOOK 4

ELANA JOHNSON

AEJ
CREATIVE WORKS

ISBN-13: 978-1-953506-07-8

"Trent, party of two?"

Trent Baker stood, wondering if he could get out of this date before it really started. Kathy was a brunette—his only requirement for his friends, who had been setting him up on dates for a couple of months now—but she wasn't anything like the kind of woman he wanted to spend more than five minutes with.

He knew, because they'd been waiting for a table at the steakhouse for twenty minutes and he'd stopped talking halfway through.

But he didn't ask Kathy for a raincheck, because he'd never cash that in. And she didn't act like she wanted to leave either. Maybe she just wanted ribs or the killer delicious rolls at Stan's.

Trent thought at least he'd eat well tonight, but he wouldn't be getting a second date.

Kathy carried the conversation, and Trent felt himself loosening up a little bit as drinks came, and then main dishes. He laughed with her when a couple on the dance floor started doing a professional swing and took a long drink from his soda, thinking maybe he just needed to open his mind to women he didn't immediately click with.

Her phone went off, and she said, "Do you mind?"

"Go ahead." He had his phone on the table too, because his six-year-old son, Porter, could need him at any moment.

Of course, his sister who watched the boy had never interrupted one of Trent's dates yet. But Kathy didn't know that, so Trent's phone sat on the table, screen up.

Kathy twittered over something on her device, and she looked up and said, "It's my boyfriend."

Boyfriend.

The word echoed through Trent's head, and he blinked at the woman across from him. Her thumbs flew across the screen and the look of joy on her face couldn't be anything but sincere.

"Boyfriend?" Trent finally asked, employing his police officer voice. Maybe not the one he used on his four German shepherds while he worked on their K9 training, but close.

Very close.

Kathy looked up, surprise on her face. "Yeah, Bruce?"

As if Trent should know who Bruce was. Trent had been back in Hawthorne Harbor for four years, and sure, he worked for the police department. But he certainly didn't know every citizen in town.

"How long have you and Bruce been dating?" Trent put his napkin on the table, ready to flee this disaster. Ready to simply be a single dad for the rest of his life. He could raise Porter. He could. He could find some way to ease the loneliness in his life. He could.

But he wasn't going out with another woman from this town.

"Oh, six or seven months." Kathy put her phone down and beamed at him.

"What did you think this was?" Trent waved between the two of them and leaned his elbows on the table.

She blinked, confusion racing through her eyes. "Oh, no." She covered her mouth with one hand. "Did you think this was a date?"

Trent refrained from rolling his eyes by looking up at the waiter as he arrived. "We're ready to go," he said, already pulling out his wallet.

"So no dessert?"

Trent threw a few twenty-dollar bills on the table and stood. "No dessert." The woman had gotten her steak and salad bar already.

"Trent," she said, but he was already walking toward the front door. He had to drive her home—he wasn't going to be rude or anything—but he didn't have to stay in public for this conversation.

Embarrassment and frustration heated his face, and

though autumn had arrived in Hawthorne Harbor, Trent felt hot from head to toe.

Thankfully, Kathy caught up to him and got in his truck without further incident.

"Georgia said she had a friend who needed a friend."

Trent grunted, not sure how to respond. Friends who went out together paid for their own meals. They didn't dress up in bright pink sundresses, wear heels, or put on as much makeup as Kathy had.

Of course, he barely knew her. Maybe she did dress like this all the time.

"It's fine," he said, practically jamming his foot to the floor in his haste to get this date over with. "I don't want to talk about it."

The drive to her house took eight minutes. Eight painfully long minutes of silence, and Trent didn't get out to walk her to the door. After all, her *boyfriend* was probably waiting just inside.

"Thank you for dinner," she said, and Trent nodded her right out of the truck. He watched to make sure she got inside, as darkness had fallen and the police officer in him wouldn't let him just drive off.

But then he did pull out of her driveway and head down the highway toward the coast.

He didn't want to go back to Eliza's and explain anything to her, and the date had only lasted one hour and fifteen minutes, including that awkward drive.

His sister would ask a lot of questions and then start

scrolling through her phone for more of her single friends. And Trent had already tried with three of them, and nothing had clicked.

"Maybe nothing ever will," he said to himself and the night in front of him. "Maybe Savannah was your click." The very thought of his wife made his heart pinch.

But he'd spent a year in complete mourning, barely alive, barely there for his toddler. And he wasn't going back to that person. Savannah wouldn't want him to anyway.

Maybe coming back to Hawthorne Harbor was a bad idea, he thought.

But his sister lived here, and his parents were just a few minutes away in Bell Hill. He'd needed their help with Porter, and their support in everything after Savannah's death.

He'd been lucky to get a spot on the police force, and his experience from the international airport in Seattle had sealed the job for him.

Cheery, yellow light caught his attention, and he realized he'd driven all the way up to Magleby Mansion. A party was clearly in full swing, and Trent felt like he was living inside a bubble.

Other people had fun. Great first dates. Boyfriends and girlfriends. But he just had his K9 dogs, his son, and his monotonous day-after-day job.

He wanted *more* than that, but at the same time, he was comfortable with the life he had.

Maybe that was why dating stung so much. It reminded him of how far out of his comfort zone he had to get in order to start and maintain a relationship.

He turned into the circular lane to turn around, a truck with a construction rack on it catching his attention.

"Michaels Construction," he read to himself. He eased on the brake and stopped, snapping a quick picture of the side of the truck so he could call and get a quote on what it would take in terms of time and money to build a deck off the back of his house.

If there was anything he loved more than his son and his K9 dogs, it was his back yard. All it was missing at this point, after four years of Trent's hard work, was a deck.

But he wasn't going to call Michael on Friday night. He didn't need to add insult to injury.

HE CALLED the construction company on Monday morning and got a Lauren who scheduled a time for the general contractor to come out to Trent's house to take measurements, talk dimensions, and get the information he needed to provide a quote.

Trent had the whole day off, and with his son in school, he found himself out in the yard with all four German shepherds under his care.

He threw them a ball for about thirty minutes before all of them found the shade from the three giant Washington hawthorn trees he cultivated along the side of his back yard.

All four dogs panted, their huge tongues lolling out of their mouths while Trent pruned and weeded, hopefully for the last time before winter set in.

"Hello?" a woman called, and Trent startled away from the rose bushes. Wilson stood, and Trent held out his hand for the dog to stay.

"In the back," he said, moving toward the fence to unlatch it.

He rounded the corner of the house and came face-to-face with the prettiest woman he'd seen in years. And years.

She had long, dark hair she'd pulled into a ponytail which draped over her shoulder, and she looked at him with sparkly, dark eyes that made his breath catch somewhere behind his lungs.

"I'm Lauren Michaels," she said, extending her hand for him to shake over the chest-high chainlink.

Trent fumbled the latch, his heart also tossing around inside his chest.

"Lauren Michaels," he said, understanding dawning on him as he finally got the fence open. "I'm Trent Baker."

He shook her hand, enjoying the zing as their skin met. He had so many questions for her, and none of them were about the deck.

The biggest one—and one he'd really need to know before this woman left his property—was, *Do you have a boyfriend?*

"How do you feel about dogs?" he asked, keeping himself between her and the rest of the yard.

"I love dogs," Lauren said, trying not to admire this man quite so much. But he clearly spent time in a gym— and the yard, if the work gloves were any indication—and he had beautiful brown hair and a pair of eyes to match.

He wore a T-shirt that strained across his chest and biceps, and while Lauren had known who Trent was the moment he'd called, it was clear he didn't know who she was.

Or even that she *was* a *she*. It was a common mistake, what with her last name being a common first name for men. Still, it had an S on it, but somehow people overlooked that a lot.

"So I have four German shepherds back here," he said as he finally started walking into the yard. "They're police dogs, and they only respond to me. They shouldn't even approach you. And you can't approach them until I say." He cast her a quick glance that held kindness and apprehension, along with the power and authority in his voice. "Okay?"

"Sounds great," Lauren said, following him and wondering if she could ask him out again. Did she really want to get her heart sliced again by this man?

He doesn't remember, she told herself, but she honestly wasn't sure if that was better or not. His wife had just passed away, and Lauren hadn't known that. No wonder Trent Baker had no recollection of her first, flubbed attempt to get a date with him.

She waited near the back door, which had a few steps leading down to the yard and he definitely needed more for this stunning space. From the dwarf apple trees to the lavender growing along the house, to the grape vines to the stunning hawthorns on the far side of the yard—where the dogs waited—Trent definitely needed a deck to enjoy all of his hard work.

Trent kept walking and he spoke to the dogs in low tones so that Lauren couldn't tell what he was saying. He finally turned and gestured for her to come on over. She did, glad when only one of the shepherds came with him as he approached her. She liked dogs, sure, but maybe not four sixty-pounders at the same time.

"This is Wilson," Trent said, and he yipped at the dog before it came trotting forward to greet Lauren.

Wilson sniffed and she crouched down to give the dog a healthy pat around his jowls and ears. "Oh, you're just a big softie, aren't you? I bet your dad lets you sleep on the bed and everything." She grinned up at Trent, stunned again by his good looks.

So maybe she'd been glad she hadn't run into him in three years, but that didn't mean she couldn't try again. Did it? He was single, she knew that. Not really into dating, from what she'd heard.

But she wasn't in the gossip circles much and could only rely on what she heard from Gillian. And Gillian had a long-time boyfriend and didn't know as much as she used to. Other than her, Lauren spent all of her time with men, and they certainly didn't know the last time Trent had gone out with someone.

One by one, each dog came over and got some love from Lauren, and she caught Trent looking at her with a strange glint in his eye. She couldn't interpret it before she cleared her throat and got back to business.

"So, tell me about this deck." She turned to survey the open area at the back of the house. "How big are you thinking?" She pulled her tape measure from her tool belt and flicked it out.

She was the best general contractor in town, but she didn't work nearly as much as some of the other companies. She didn't want to think it was because of her gender, but she couldn't think of any other reason.

Trent detailed the kind of paradise he wanted, and Lauren could see it come to life in her mind.

She used her tablet and the expensive construction software she'd bought to draw up some quick plans as he took the dogs inside to get them a fresh bowl of water.

Twenty minutes later, Lauren felt confident she could tap "generate" and her tablet would give her a timeline as well as a quote for this dreamy man she really wanted to work with.

She didn't need to ask him out today if she could land this job. And the truth was, she needed another big project once she finished the wing up at Magleby Mansion.

"So where are we at?" he asked, coming down the steps and exhaling heavily. "My son will be done at school soon, and I have to go pick him up."

Lauren's chest squeezed on the word *son*, but she didn't let it show. "I can email this to you." She raised her eyebrows in a silent question.

He joined her at her side, the scent of his skin hitting her like a heavenly punch of cologne and sweat. She kept the swoon under control, but his voice rumbled through her when he said, "I have time. Let me see it." He peered at her tablet, and Lauren reminded herself to get the job done.

"Okay." She cleared her throat, wishing he didn't make her so nervous. Maybe if she'd gone out with anyone whose name she could remember in the past three years, her heart wouldn't be hammering quite so hard right now.

She detailed the project, the hawthorn wood she'd use to mirror the trees, the swing, the benches, the place for the permanent umbrella to be secured so the bay winds wouldn't disrupt his back yard barbeques.

"And what does this cost?" he asked, taking a step back. "It's beautiful. Exactly what I want. I just...." He gave a chuckle that sounded nervous. "I'm on a budget."

"Of course," Lauren said. "We can do three payments. One-third up front. One in the middle. And one at the end once you're one-hundred-percent satisfied with my work."

Their eyes met, and Lauren wasn't sure if she was hallucinating or not, but she felt a quick spark of attraction between them. Fine, it was more like a lightning bolt.

Could he feel it too?

The seconds stretched, and she finally shook herself out of the depths of his eyes. "Here's the price and timeline." She tapped the button and the drawings changed to the quote. She handed him the tablet and stepped back. "I have to finish my great-aunt's place first, so I'm not available until probably the end of October."

And then she had the Festival of Trees after that. She opened her mouth to say she couldn't start until the new year when Trent said, "This looks great," and handed back her tablet. "You're hired."

Happiness flowed through Lauren, and not just because she'd gotten another job to keep her in business for another few months. She'd learned to take things day by day, month by month. Doing that, she'd kept Michaels Construction in business for six years.

"Is your great-aunt Mabel Magleby?"

"That's right." Lauren tapped a few more buttons and added, "I'll get this printed. Do you want to stop by my place to sign it? Or I can bring it over here at your convenience." She was so professional, and while she might want to take Trent to lunch, she also wanted him to recommend her to all of his friends who might need something done, whether it be a bathroom remodel or a new addition to their house.

"I can come to you." He smiled, and honestly, such an action on such a handsome face should be illegal.

"Great." Lauren stood there, though she had no reason to stay for another second. And Trent needed to go get his son, but he didn't move either. Perhaps the lightning had struck him too.

"What's Mabel doing up there?" he asked.

"A complete renovation of the west wing," Lauren said, seizing onto an opportunity and hoping she didn't mess it up. "She's having a big party for the reopening. You should come." She added a smile to her face, thinking her invitation could be interpreted as friendly. Like, *Hey, the whole town is invited, so you should come.*

She started for the corner of the house and the fence, but he said, "Lauren?"

Lauren turned back to him. "Yeah?"

"Have we met before?" He tilted his head, those eyes harboring so much intelligence.

Lauren wanted to deny it, but she also really wanted a second chance with him. So she let herself emit a light laugh—not a giggle. A businesswoman such as herself did *not* giggle—and toss her ponytail over her shoulder.

"I asked you out once," she said with a quick one-shoulder shrug. "I didn't think you remembered that."

Trent looked like she'd thrown a glass of ice water in his face. "I don't remember that. When was it?"

"Oh, I don't know. Three or four years ago."

Something dark crossed his face, and Lauren took it as her cue to leave. "It was no big deal." She rounded the corner and had her hand on the latch when he practically yelled her name.

He came around the corner, almost colliding with her. She blinked at him, all the shadows gone from his eyes. She really hoped her invitation to dinner four years ago wouldn't jeopardize this deck now. She not only needed the job, she really wanted to work on this specific project.

"I'd like to take you up on your offer," he said. "That is, if you don't have a boyfriend." He reached up and rubbed his hand up the back of his neck in the most adorable way.

Lauren's face burst into a smile. "I don't have a boyfriend."

Trent grinned too. "Great. So I'll stop by and sign those papers and we'll chat then. I really am late to get my son."

"I'll be at the Mansion most of the day tomorrow, if you want to stop by up there." Lauren didn't usually feel so shy—as evidenced by her bold move to ask out the new bachelor in town all those years ago—but somehow, in this small patch of lawn, with Trent, she did.

"I'll see if I can get up there," he said. "I'm on duty tomorrow."

Lauren nodded and got her slightly shaky legs to get her off his property and back to her office before she blew her second chance with the deliciously handsome Trent Baker.

3

Trent sat in the parent pick-up line, his heart thumping in some strange way it hadn't in so long, he couldn't even identify what kind of beat it was.

But he knew it had everything to do with the beautiful Lauren Michaels. Had she really asked him out before? How could he have forgotten a woman like her?

He'd almost texted his sister to find out if she remembered Lauren, but he didn't need her asking questions. And Eliza would. She was as keen as their mother, and the last thing Trent needed was either one of them asking about his love life.

When he'd picked up Porter on Friday night, Eliza had asked, "So?" and all Trent had been able to do was shake his head. He'd tell her about Kathy's *boyfriend* eventually, but Trent didn't need to relive the humiliation right now.

The back door of the SUV opened, and Trent put on his daddy smile. "Hey, bud, how was school?"

Porter climbed into the backseat, his backpack huge and getting stuck on the top of the doorframe. He yanked on it and finally settled in the middle of the bench seat.

"Joey brought a lizard," he said, his voice high and full of excitement. "And Miss Terry chose three people to hold it, and I got to!"

"That's great, bud." Trent eased the truck out of the line and into the drive-through lane. "What was the lizard's name?"

"Chicken."

Trent scoffed. "What?" He glanced in the rear-view mirror and met Porter's eyes. At least they were his and not Savannah's. No, Trent saw her in the shape of his son's face, the roundness of his nose, and the way everything seemed to be made of magic. Including, apparently, lizards named Chicken.

"Yeah, Chicken," Porter said.

"Put your seatbelt on, bud." Trent stopped at the sign before pulling out of the school driveway and waited for his son to click his buckle.

"I guess lizards are born from eggs," Porter said. "And Joey thought that it would be a chicken, so he named it Chicken even after it was hatched."

"Okay, then." Trent turned toward Main Street, wondering if it was too early to grab dinner. Then he wouldn't have to leave the house again that night. He wondered when he'd become an old soul, as a thirty-seven-year-old shouldn't want to eat dinner at three-thirty in the afternoon.

"Are you hungry, Porty?"

"No, it was Baylor's birthday, and his mom brought doughnuts." He just looked out the window, but Trent felt like someone had stabbed a toothpick into his heart.

He hadn't been able to take a treat into Porter's class last year, because he'd been on duty. This year, he'd already put in for a vacation day in March, so he could be Mister Mom and take cupcakes to Porter's classmates.

"Maybe we could grab sandwiches and take the canines to the beach."

"Will you teach me that word for find?" Porter asked.

"Yeah. You can work on it with Tornado. He's still trying to learn it."

"Wilson always takes over."

"Yeah, well, Wilson is the pack leader." Trent turned down Main Street. "Pick a place, and we'll stop and get something and go."

Trent took the dogs everywhere with him. Sometimes he leashed one or two and made them work among pedestrians. Wilson and Pecorino had performed brilliantly at the Lavender Festival a few months ago, and then Trent had paired Wilson with Brutus for the Fall Festival.

Tornado was still a bit excitable, but he'd done really well with Lauren. *That's because Lauren has calm energy,*

Trent thought. As he'd been working with his police dogs —and taking training courses from the K9 Unit in Seattle —he'd learned a lot about a person's energy.

And Tornado hadn't whined once with Lauren, so she definitely possessed an energy that spoke to Tornado's.

"Pizza," Porter said as Trent drove by The Slice. Simple things like that used to frustrate him, but now he just flipped around and parked across the street. If his son wanted pizza, they'd get pizza.

Trent held his son's hand as they crossed the street—properly, in the crosswalk. He didn't need anything getting back to his boss that he wasn't a law-abiding citizen when he wasn't on duty.

They joined the line for family night pizza, and by the time they had their two boxes and were ready to head to the beach, the sun was already sinking fast. Trent sighed. He really disliked winter, and it seemed like the season was nearly upon them.

As he set the pizza boxes on the seat on the passenger side and then turned to move around the front of his truck, his eyes caught a flyer taped to the lamppost.

"Magleby Mansion grand unveiling," he read aloud. He pulled down the paper and searched for the date. It was next weekend, and he heard Lauren's voice saying, "You should come. You should come."

Surely she didn't mean as her date, but when Trent thought about those few charged moments in his back yard, his thoughts turned muddy.

He folded the flyer and put it in his back pocket before he got behind the wheel. He'd simply ask her tomorrow when he went to sign the work contract.

The beach brought relief to his soul in a way that nothing else could. Savannah had loved the sound of the surf, the feel of sand against her bare feet, and watching the sun sink into the waves.

Trent had tolerated the beach while she'd been alive, but now he treasured his time there, especially when he went with Porter. He felt closer to her there than anywhere else, and he often told his son stories about her while they ate or threw a Frisbee for the dogs.

Tonight, Trent felt weary though he hadn't even put on his uniform and gone into work. He sighed as he sank onto the blanket he kept in the back of the truck.

"Wait," he told the dogs, who quivered with anticipation of running out into the waves. Several other canines ran around the sand, but Trent's dogs couldn't go until he released them. And they better come back as soon as he whistled.

Wilson sat, which helped Pecorino and Brutus to do the same. "Tornado," Trent said as if he didn't care at all if the dog sat or not. But he did, and Trent said, "Yep."

All four dogs sprinted toward the ocean, with Tornado barking every other step. Trent shook his head and laughed as they met the water and sent splashes several feet into the air.

"Your mom used to make the best chocolate mint

brownies," he said to Porter as the boy opened the lid on the first pizza box. "And we never came to the beach without them, even though I used to tease her that they'd melt."

Porter picked up a piece of pizza and paused before he took a bite. "Do you know how to make the brownies?"

"I have her recipes, yeah." But Trent hadn't made any of them. He made boxed macaroni and cheese, or spaghetti, or hamburgers and hot dogs. Savannah used to make delicious pasta casseroles and the best soups and stews on the planet. But Trent hadn't been able to bring himself to pull out her binder and look at her handwriting as she made adjustments to the measurements or left herself notes for what to do next time she made the dish.

Because it was too painful of a reminder that there would be no next time.

"We should make them," Porter said. "Maybe for Aunt Eliza's birthday."

"Yeah." Trent ate and kept watch over the dogs while the sun sank. When they had just enough time to get back to the truck before it was too dark to see, he packed up and took his son home.

THE NEXT DAY, TRENT SHOWED UP TO WORK TO FIND ADAM Herrin in a less-than-joyful mood. "What's up with him?"

Trent asked out of the side of his mouth. Sarah, Adam's personal secretary, glared at the Police Chief's door. "Oh, someone called and asked about the security plan for the Festival of Trees, and you know how the Chief feels about that."

Trent did know, and he also understood Adam's frustration. "The Fall Festival ended ten days ago."

"That's exactly what Adam said." Sarah gave Trent's hand a pat. "How's Porter?"

"He's doing great." Trent started to move over to his desk, hoping he didn't have any paperwork to deal with from his day off.

"Didn't you have a date over the weekend?" Sarah asked, and Trent cringed. He'd enlisted almost everyone around him to help him find a girlfriend, and while it had sounded like a good idea at the time, now Trent was really regretting it.

"Yeah, it isn't going to work out."

"I have a neighbor—"

"I think I'm going to try it on my own for a while." Trent gave Sarah a smile he hoped would soften his words. He wasn't sure if he was saying he'd find his own dates or if he'd just like to stop dating for a while.

Until Lauren Michaels had shown up at his house yesterday afternoon, Trent would've chosen never going out again. But she had him reconsidering his decision.

Thankfully, he only had a couple of reports on his

desk, and he flew through them before heading outside to work with his German shepherds.

As he set up a new "bomb" for Tornado to find, Chief Herrin came through the gate. "You got a minute, Trent?" he asked.

"Sure thing, Chief." Trent paused in his prep.

"I'd like you to run point on the Festival of Trees security," Adam said without looking away from Trent. "How do you feel about that?"

Pride swelled in Trent's chest. "Sure thing."

"I need a report by the end of the week." He finally glanced around the dog training arena. "I know it'll take you from this more than you'd like. But with Janey pregnant, I'm not sure I can handle another event right now."

"Janey's pregnant?" Trent rarely knew any town news, and he grinned at his boss and good friend. "That's good news, right?"

"It is, yeah." Adam smiled back. "But she's high-risk, and I'm trying to juggle things at home, and with Jess...." He blew out his breath. "I can't take on the Festival of Trees."

"I've worked it for three years, boss. I can do it." Trent really wanted to do a good job, not just for Adam, but to feel like he was doing something good with his life.

He'd never struggled before Savannah passed away, but now he felt like he really needed to make something of his life. The problem was, he didn't know how, and often simply reverted to keeping Porter fed and bathed, his yard and garden in tip-top shape, and tried to get his dogs to find trace amounts of explosives in pull toys.

He was comfortable in his life, and heading up the team for the Festival of Trees would pull him from that comfort zone.

And so would going out with Lauren Michaels.

4

Lauren tried not to watch the clock, but when her foreman, Gene, left and then returned to Magleby Mansion, Lauren couldn't help the restlessness in her muscles.

When would Trent show up?

His paperwork sat in her truck, because she'd been secretly planning to get him alone and ask him to the unveiling for real. As her date.

Aunt Mabel had made it clear Lauren should bring someone, and that the article about the new west wing in the Mansion would be printed in every magazine and paper from here to Forks.

Lauren had added fifteen minutes to her treadmill workout that morning in anticipation of being photographed. And to have one of Hawthorne Harbor's most eligible—and handsome—bachelors on her arm? Lauren definitely needed to go shopping for a new dress.

But first, Trent needed to show up to sign his contract so she could ask him.

It felt like hours later when she heard a dog bark. Her heart leapt, and she forced herself to casually move over to the window so she could see if a certain man had arrived with his four doggy pals.

Sure enough, Trent stood at the tailgate of his truck, talking to the four dogs who sat in two perfect rows, apparently listening to him.

Lauren smiled at the sight but moved away from the window before anyone saw her standing there. She'd already confessed that she'd asked him out once. She didn't need to broadcast that her old feelings had grown new life as soon as she'd seen him fumbling with that fence.

And seeing him standing at the back of his truck in his police uniform? Lauren had zero defense against this man.

It seemed to take him forever to make it upstairs, and when he did, he said, "Wow, this place is completely different."

She watched him gaze around the room where she worked. "We're on the finishing touches," she said, drinking in the width of his shoulders in that uniform. Wow. Just wow. "Paint and molding. Then Aunt Mabel has the furniture and art pieces coming in."

He lifted his hand like he could reach the chandelier, which of course, he couldn't. "I saw a flyer for the unveiling." He met her eye and didn't look away. "I don't have to work that night, so if the invitation still stands, I'd love to come."

"The whole town is invited," Lauren said, immediately wishing she could recall the words.

Trent took a step toward her, and her fingers tightened around the paint roller she held. "I was thinking you and I could go together," he said. "I won't bring my son. We could go to dinner beforehand, if you'd like."

Lauren controlled the rate her smile spread her lips. "I do need a date. Aunt Mabel is planning a big to-do, with a photographer, as I found out this morning, for all these articles she's procured."

"Ah, I see. So you need me to hang on your arm." He spoke in a playful voice that set every one of Lauren's nerves on fire.

"If you want the job for one night," she said with a shrug, trying to control her pulse. But her heart seemed to be in a race for its life. "Dinner will be served here, and I'd love for you to come and eat with me, dance with me, stand next to me while the photographers take pictures."

Trent's smile was slow and easy and absolutely devastating. "I'd like that. You know what will happen if I do that, right?"

Lauren frowned at him. "No. What?"

"With articles and pictures published in newspapers and magazines?"

"Yeah," Lauren said slowly.

"You don't spend much time with other women."

Lauren's defenses flew into place, and everything she'd fought against as a female general contractor reared its ugly head. "So what?"

"So you don't understand what kind of gossip that will start." He settled his weight on his back leg. "I don't mind. I've...." He swallowed, and Lauren was glad she wasn't the only one who was nervous.

"I'd like to go out with you," he said. "I'm sorry I didn't respond well last time. I don't even remember it. But I... don't really remember a whole lot for that first year after my wife died."

Lauren nodded. "It was bad timing, obviously."

"And for full disclosure, my last, oh, ten dates have been disasters. So I can't promise anything more than that."

Lauren laughed, but Trent just gazed at her, that handsome smile on his lips. "Oh, you're serious." Lauren sobered and wanted to give him a date that wasn't a disaster.

"I'm afraid so." Trent stuck his hands in his pockets and shrugged.

"Well, I'd still very much like to go out with you," she said. "We can go earlier than the unveiling, if you'd like. That way, if we don't get along, you won't have to endure the gossip." Lauren really hoped they'd get along, because if he wasn't the one on her arm, she wouldn't even know who to ask.

"Oh, I don't think we need to worry about getting along." Trent gave her an easy smile. "Let me look at my work schedule and talk to my sister. Maybe I can get your number and let you know?"

"Your sister?" Lauren asked, wondering where she'd even left her phone.

"She watches Porter for me when I go out." Trent extracted his phone from his pocket and looked at her expectantly.

She dictated her number for him, and he said, "I sent you a text."

"Great. When I find my phone, I'll add you."

"And just to be sure, you really don't have a boyfriend, right?"

Lauren heard the insecurity in his voice, and she shook her head. "No boyfriend." Not for at least five years. But she kept that to herself. Trent didn't need to know about her "marriage" to her company, as her last boyfriend had accused her of.

"It's a semi-formal event," she said. "I'm wearing a fancy dress."

His eyes slid down her body, and Lauren felt every inch of his gaze. "Will you be wearing heels?" he asked.

"Probably."

"Can I wear my uniform? Is that formal enough?"

"Of course." The very idea of having his uniformed presence next to her at the unveiling next week had her stomach shaking. She finally remembered why he'd come to the Mansion. "I have your contract in my truck."

She set her paint roller in the tray and stepped in front of him, very aware of the nearness of him as he followed her downstairs.

"Lauren?" Aunt Mabel stepped out of the ballroom before Lauren could leave the Mansion. Her gaze flickered to Trent. "Hello, Trent. What are you doing here?"

"I'm hiring Lauren to do my back deck," he said, keeping a healthy distance between them. "You're looking good." He stepped over to Mabel and gave her a quick kiss on the cheek. "The west wing looks beautiful."

"That's all Lauren," Mabel said, a glint in her eye that Lauren recognized. A matchmaking glint. Little did Aunt Mabel know that Lauren had managed to get a date on her own this time.

"The contract is in my truck," she said. "Then I'll get right back to painting."

"Oh, the paint can wait." Mabel turned and started back into the ballroom. "Come try the cheesecakes for the unveiling. Trent, you can too, if you have time."

Lauren wanted to spend more time with him, but she didn't want to do it under the watchful eye of her great aunt.

"Thank you, Mabel," he said diplomatically without committing to anything and followed Lauren outside.

"You don't have to stay," she said. "Can I pat the dogs today?" She got the contract out of her glove box and handed it to him.

"Sure, go ahead."

She gave all four dogs a good rub while he signed and initialed. "How'd you learn to train dogs?" she asked.

"I've taken classes from K9 Units," he said. "Went to Chicago for a three-week intensive training and just started doing it."

Lauren nodded and took the contract back. "I'll start sourcing the supplies," she said. "Payment on the first day."

"I've got it here." He pulled a slip of paper from his back pocket and handed it to her.

She took the check without looking at it. "Great. Thank you."

"Tell your aunt thank you, but I can't stay."

Simultaneous disappointment and relief hit Lauren in the chest. "I'll tell her. Thanks for driving up here."

"Oh, it got me out of the office." He smiled at her and walked around his truck to the driver's door. "Say good-bye to the pretty lady, guys."

One of the dogs barked, and Trent grinned at her before getting in his truck and driving away.

Lauren watched him go, a blissful sigh slipping through her lips even as her pulse rioted. He'd asked her out. She really hoped he could arrange everything with his son so they could go out before the unveiling, because

two weeks was entirely too long to wait to see Trent
again.

"What are you looking at?"

Lauren spun to find Gene standing on the top step.
"Nothing."

"There's paint drying in a tray upstairs."

"I just had a new client come sign his paperwork," she
said. "And now my aunt wants me to taste cheesecake.
Then I'll get back to painting."

Gene looked down the drive again, as if Lauren had
lied about what she was looking at. She marched past
him, determined to keep her crush on the gorgeous police
officer a secret for just a little longer.

Lauren arrived in the parking lot for Wedding Row
five minutes after the agreed meeting time. She didn't
want to be here, but when Gillian's enthusiastic face filled
her window, Lauren couldn't help laughing.

"Come on," Gillian said as Lauren opened her door
and got out. "We're buying a dress today." Gillian spoke
like buying a dress was akin to winning a million dollars.

But Lauren didn't have a date with Trent on the horizon, and the last thing she wanted to spend her Saturday
morning on was shopping. But the unveiling was only a
week away, and it seemed like that would be the next time
she saw Trent.

So she better get something to really wow him. He had texted a little bit, but he wasn't particularly loquacious and didn't seem interested in using his device to get to know her or reveal anything about himself.

Gillian linked her arm through Lauren's. "Come on, girl. Maybe you'll meet your knight in shining armor next week."

"Maybe," Lauren said, a twinge of guilt pulling through her. She'd kept Trent a secret from everyone, which honestly wasn't hard. Her all-male crew didn't care who she went out with. Neither did Camo, her lizard. And while she talked with Gillian every day and they'd arranged this shopping trip, Lauren hadn't said anything.

As Gillian opened the door to the wedding dress shop, Lauren felt like she'd been punched in the gut. "Do they even have party dresses here?"

"Of course they do." Gillian glided into the store as if she'd been there countless times before, which of course, she probably had. "My friend needs a dress for the Magleby Mansion unveiling next weekend," she said to a dark-haired woman, who scanned Lauren.

"Size six?"

"Yes," Lauren said, wondering how the woman knew. "It will probably have to be altered in the bust."

"We'll see." She gave Lauren a warm smile. "I'm Amanda. What colors were you thinking?"

"She's the general contractor over the whole build," Gillian said, much too loudly. "And she likes to blend in."

She nudged Lauren forward, but her face burned with embarrassment, and she'd forgotten the question.

"Are you looking to blend in or stand out?" Amanda asked, and Lauren had no idea how to answer. Aunt Mabel would probably want her to stand out.

"I guess I could wear something a little brighter."

"With your hair and skin tone, you'd look great in teal. And I happen to have something that just came in." She moved over to a rack and pulled a dress from seemingly nowhere. It had a hemline that would barely reach her knees and absolutely no straps.

"There's no way I have enough goods to hold that up," she said.

"Our seamstresses are miracle workers." Amanda folded the dress over her arm. "I have something in cream too. And this black might be perfect. It's a standout and a blend-in all in one."

They started with the teal one, and sure enough, Lauren's chest was nowhere big enough to fill it out. She also thought it was so bright she'd blind anyone who looked her way.

The cream dress fell awkwardly to her calf and had a layer of lace over the whole thing that made her feel like she was going to marry a man she'd never met.

As Amanda helped her step into the black dress, Lauren could tell this one would be perfect. It hugged her waist and flared to her knee from there, with beautiful roses that adorned the waistline.

The bust would need to be taken in, but with the thick straps over the shoulders, it at least looked like it could be altered to fit.

"And if you wore a spunky pair of colored heels, you'd steal the show."

"I want to see," Gillian called from the other side of the door, and Lauren stepped out of the oversized dressing room to show her best friend.

Gillian gasped and covered her mouth, her blue eyes flitting from Lauren's shoulder to her knee to her waist. "It's awesome, Lauren." She brushed her blonde bangs out of her eyes. "You can get it altered in time, right?"

"Of course." Amanda looked at Lauren. "Is this the one?"

"Yes," Lauren and Gillian said at the same time, and Amanda called someone over to help her pin and measure.

"You're definitely going to sweep someone off their feet," Gillian gushed as Lauren stepped up to the counter to pay.

"I've already got a date," Lauren said, deciding that since shopping had been so easy, she'd share her secret with Gillian.

"You what?" Gillian stepped to Lauren's side and stared at her until Lauren turned toward her. "Who is it?"

Lauren flicked her gaze to the clerk, who could certainly calculate tax and listen at the same time. So she gave a quick shake of her head, a system of communicating she and Gillian had worked out long ago.

As soon as they hit the sidewalk, Gillian said, "Girl, you better start talking."

Lauren gathered her hair into a ponytail and said, "I think I want a burger for lunch."

"No way." Gillian shook her head. "They're altering the bust on that dress. Not the waist."

Lauren couldn't argue, so she went into the trendy bistro with Gillian and stuck to the salad side of the menu. They'd barely ordered before Gillian asked, "So who are you going to the unveiling with?"

"Promise not to tell? Or act weird. Or shriek," Lauren tacked onto the end.

Gillian looked offended. "I would never shriek in a bistro."

Lauren shook her head, holding onto Trent's name just a little longer. Right when it looked like Gillian would launch herself across the table and throttle her, Lauren said, "It's Trent Baker."

Gillian shrieked, just as Lauren expected, drawing the interest of everyone in the bistro on that busy Saturday.

"Gillian," Lauren hissed, heat rushing to her face. How was she going to handle the press? Or the gossip once everyone in town saw her and Trent together?

"How did this happen?" Gillian had never looked so alive. "I mean, you asked him out years ago and he said no."

"He actually didn't say anything," Lauren said, the memory of her first invitation as vivid in her mind as if she'd done it yesterday. "He said he doesn't remember me asking him. He'd just returned to town after the death of his first wife. I shouldn't have even asked." She shrugged like she hadn't thought about his rejection for months afterward.

"I just can't...Trent Baker." Gillian spoke as if the man was the white whale, untouchable somehow. "And how are we feeling about his son?"

Lauren hadn't let herself think about it too much. "I don't know. I don't even know if Trent and I will make it past one date. He said the last ten he's been on have been disasters."

"Yeah, because the last woman he went out with was Kathy Winston."

"What? She's been dating Bruce for months. Oh." Suddenly his obsessive questions about her having a boyfriend made so much sense. Her heart beat out sympathy for the man, and she spent lunch detailing how she and Trent had agreed to attend the unveiling together.

Even with the shopping, it honestly was one of the best Saturdays of her life. So far. Because next Saturday would hopefully be the one where she and Trent made a love connection.

5

Trent could barely find a spare minute to eat, let alone make time for a date with Lauren. He disliked that, but he wanted to do a good job on the Festival of Trees security plan for Chief Herrin, so he devoted his time to that, helping Porter get his letters going the right way, and taking care of the dogs.

By the time the new week rolled around, Trent went over the plan with Lou one more time, then Jason, and finally, he knocked on the Chief's door.

"Yep."

Trent found Adam behind his desk, his fingers twisting a Rubix cube. The man didn't even look at the puzzle, just turned and flipped the cube while he gazed at Trent.

"You okay, Chief?" Trent knew Adam completed Rubix cubes when he had particularly difficult problems to work through. Trent's yard was so immaculate for the same reason. He couldn't stand to be idle, because being inside his mind wasn't that great of a place to be.

"Just thinking," Adam said, setting the cube on the edge of his desk. "You've got the plan?" He extended his hand to take the folder of information Trent had prepared.

He passed it over and took a seat across from the Chief. "We'll need six additional men," Trent said. "I figured that was okay, because we've hired seasonally for our festivals before."

"Yeah." Adam sounded distracted as he flipped pages. There was no way he was actually reading what was on them. "There's a meeting with the director tomorrow," he said. "Ten-thirty. At the community center."

"I'll be there," Trent said. "I've got this, Chief."

Adam handed the folder back, and Trent took it, stood, and left the office. He settled at his own desk and went over his plan one more time.

Uniformed officers prevented the most problems, but the public didn't appreciate feeling like they were being watched. So he had two pairs of officers on duty for the duration of the festival. One pair would walk the festivities at any given time. The other two would be in a back room, watching on closed-circuit monitors. An additional, plain-clothes cop would be roving during the festival as well, and all the additional cops would be to direct traffic, check bags as patrons entered, and keep the rest of

Hawthorne Harbor functioning during the month-long event.

Not only that, but the graveyard shift would drive by the community center at least twice a night, as the caller who'd asked about the security was worried about vandalism during off-hours.

Why they were, Trent didn't know. He'd grown up in nearby Bell Hill, and he'd never heard of the Festival of Trees having a vandalism problem. Sure, he'd left for just over a decade, but he'd been back in town for four years, and again, the festivals usually ran without a hitch.

That's because of plans like this, he thought, closing the folder and clicking to get his computer open. Perhaps he should do a bit more research about who he'd be meeting with tomorrow. While he'd worked the festival for the past three years, he wasn't the point man and therefore, had simply done what Adam had assigned him to do.

"Mitch Magleby," he murmured, the connection firing in his mind. Of course the Magleby's would be involved in the festival. They had their hand in almost everything in the town, as they were one of the oldest—and wealthiest—families in Hawthorne Harbor.

His thoughts drifted to Lauren, and how she hadn't grown up here. He wondered where she was from and what had brought her here—besides the family connection. There had to be bigger cities for someone with a job like hers. After all, Hawthorne Harbor didn't have a booming construction business, with new homes going in anywhere. If there was a new build, it was isolated and on family land.

He wondered what she was doing that day, and he sent off a quick text. *Do you have time for lunch today?*

Crazy at the Mansion, she sent back. But tomorrow I have a meeting in town at ten-thirty. We could go after that.

Trent stared at his phone. *Ten-thirty? Are you meeting with Mitch about the Festival of Trees?*

Yeah, that's right... How did you know?

I'll be there. Trent smiled but didn't add anything to indicate so in his text. *I'm in charge of all the security for the events.*

I build all their sets.

Trent glanced around like texting was a crime and one of his fellow officers would arrest him for it. *And you're going to build my deck too?* he sent. *If you don't have time to do it, we can postpone it.*

I have time, she sent. And I love the clam chowder at The Anchor.

Trent chuckled, which definitely drew the attention of Sarah a few desks away. The woman had ears and eyes like a hawk.

Great, see you then. Trent stuffed his phone away after that, and he managed to keep himself at his desk, clicking around on the computer and doing nothing for fifteen more minutes before he stood and said, "I'll be with the dogs."

No one even acknowledged him. Since he wasn't out

patrolling, he didn't have a partner, and the office was empty most of the time. Only during shift changes did things get lively in the police station. Or when Adam brought in food.

Didn't matter. Trent had gotten used to non-lively. He actually liked it. But a thread of excitement wove through him as he thought about seeing Lauren and taking her to lunch the next day.

"Let's hope it's not a disaster," he said to Wilson, who cocked his head because he didn't understand that command.

TRENT CAUGHT A WHIFF OF SOMETHING FLORAL MIXED WITH something like lumber as soon as he entered the community center.

Lauren was here, and dang if his heartbeat didn't jump around a bit inside his chest. So he'd had an encounter with her in the past. She didn't seem overly upset about his apparent rejection, and he'd been bold and forthright at the Mansion last week.

He found the right room for the meeting, along with at least a dozen people in attendance. Lauren sat in the front room, sandwiched between two other men. Trent recognized her foreman, Gene, as well as one of the best electricians in the county, Kameron Nash.

Trent took a seat on the end of the back row, glad he'd

made it before the meeting began. Tornado had been acting up this morning, and it had taken an hour to get him tired enough to wait for the attack command before he'd take off from the starting block.

Trent was beginning to have serious doubts about the shepherd's ability to be a police dog, but he didn't want to give up on Tornado quite yet.

Another group of people entered the room through a door in the front, and Trent recognized the pot-bellied form of Mitch Magleby. He was a generation older than Trent, but one younger than Mabel. He had the same keen eyes set in a face full of right angles and gray hair.

"Welcome, everyone," he said in a warm voice. He often played Santa Claus at town parties around the holidays, and Trent found himself smiling at the image of the man in a red suit.

"It's the sixtieth annual Festival of Trees, and we want to have a special celebration because of that."

Trent had seen the logos and special banners indicating the sixtieth anniversary of the festival on the website yesterday, but he hadn't anticipated that the festival would be any different because of that.

"We've invited people to plan special sixty-year anniversary trees, as well as anything else they want." He nodded to the woman next to him, Alecia Summers, and she flipped open her laptop.

She went through a whole presentation about the festival, when people could come set up, how much it cost to enter, and the other festivities like face-painting, food booths, and the holiday shop that would be available at the community center as well.

"We've invited the food truck owners," Mitch said. "Our construction crew." He nodded to Lauren on the front row. "And a representative from the police force to be here with us today. Now that everyone knows what and when, what do we need to talk about?"

Trent already had a plan for security, but only during the event itself. As the food truck owners talked about and organized a food truck rally for each Friday night in December, Trent realized he'd need more men in the parking lot on those nights.

Lauren said, "Construction for the festival starts in early November. All participants must submit any construction needs with their applications. At least that's how its been done in the past. Is that what we're doing this year?"

"Yes," Mitch said. "Thank you for the reminder. Alecia." She wrote something on her clipboard and looked up.

"Applications are due no later than November fifteenth," she said. "Set up begins the weekend before Thanksgiving." She searched the crowd until she found Trent. "Can we have at least one officer here during setup hours? Last year, a couple of people got pretty heated about the location of their tree."

Trent flipped open the folder he'd brought with him. "I'll add it to our plan," he said.

"We'd love a copy of that as soon as it's approved by the Chief," Mitch said. "We'd like to post it on the website this year, just so there are no bumps." He looked like he'd move to the next topic, but Trent raised his hand.

"Sorry, sir," he said. "What bumps? Just so I know how to train my men." He sounded so authoritative, and he couldn't help but notice the way Lauren twisted to look at him, a small smile on her mouth.

Mitch exchanged a glance with the third person who'd come in with him, a man who hadn't spoken yet and whose name Trent couldn't remember. "Shawn?"

The man rose, and Trent got the distinct impression he was a lawyer. Probably the one the city kept on retainer.

"We had a few complaints of vagrants hanging around the center last year." He spoke in a deep, rich voice that definitely screamed lawyer. "Moms were concerned. Some people didn't want to submit to the bag search. We had a theft from the holiday shop. A few isolated incidents over the course of the festival."

Trent nodded and asked, "Can I get your contact information? In case I have more questions or we'd like you to come speak to the crew."

"Sure." Shawn rattled it off and Trent scrawled it on the front page of his security report.

Mitch moved on to vendors for the holiday shop, their

application process, and then Alecia took over again with a short presentation on where the money from this year's Festival of Trees would be donated.

Trent's anxiety grew by the minute, because the meeting was almost over. His stomach growled. And both of those meant that he was about to go on his first date with Lauren Michaels.

6

L auren had already told Gene and Kam that she'd be eating with "a friend," so when the meeting broke up and Gene said, "Lunch at Itzel's?" a blip of frustration slipped through her.

"I'm in," Kam said. "Lauren?"

"I'm eating with someone else," she said, glad Trent had remained seated in the back row, his attention on his phone. But the man was a police officer, and she didn't believe for a minute that he didn't hear her. "But we need to meet up and talk about electrical for the Wainscott job," she said to Kam. "And let's calendar another session for after the applications are due for this festival."

Kam always had to come do some wiring to make sure the community center didn't burn to the ground during the festival.

"Will do." Kam started toward the door with Gene. "You've got my number."

Lauren watched them go, the air blowing in the community center suddenly causing a chill against her skin.

Trent looked up and their eyes met. Lauren's blood shot to a higher temperature, erasing the anxiety she'd just felt.

"You ready?" he asked in that easy-going way of his. He didn't extend his hand for her to hold, but simply stood there clutching his folder.

"Ready." She approached him. "What's in the folder?"

"My security plan. I'll need to update it with a few things."

"Have you always worked the Festival of Trees?"

"Just the past three years," he said. "I came back to Hawthorne Harbor after the death of my wife." His voice cut off and he ground it through his throat. "In February. So I've been back almost four years now, but I missed that first Festival."

Lauren nodded, her voice trapped somewhere in her chest too. "I'm sorry about your wife." She looked at him, hoping the emotion in her own voice had stayed dormant.

"Thank you," Trent said. "I have good days and bad days." He opened the door for her and stood back.

"I bet." She smiled at him as she walked outside. "What's today?"

"You know what? Today's not bad."

He hadn't said it was good either, and Lauren hoped their lunch would be something to brighten his day.

"So, I know you're not from the area," he said. "I grew up in Bell Hill and don't remember you. But the Magleby's are from here."

"Yep." Lauren popped the P at the end. "My mother is Mitch's sister. So he's my uncle. She married my dad and moved to Seattle when she was only seventeen years old." Lauren lowered her voice and said in a fake whisper, "It was somewhat of a scandal." She laughed, and Trent chuckled too.

"Seems like I've heard that story."

"Oh, everyone has," she said. "But my mom and dad are still married and still live in Seattle. I have three younger brothers who all work in the tech industry up there."

They strolled down the sidewalk, the autumn weather nice enough that Lauren didn't need a jacket but didn't feel like she'd start sweating with their leisurely pace.

"Besides, we're not the only Magleby's to have left Hawthorne Harbor."

"I'm sure you're not."

"My uncle has a brother who left when their son joined the Marines."

"Oh, right," Trent said as if he knew who she was talking about.

"His name was Hunter," Lauren said. "He's about my age. Still in the Marines." She wondered if he'd ever come back to town, but his family didn't live here anymore, so he probably wouldn't.

Of course, Lauren's family didn't live here anymore either—except for Aunt Mabel—and she'd returned.

"You came back to Hawthorne Harbor." Trent didn't phrase it as a question, but she heard the curiosity behind the words.

"That's right," she said, wondering if he'd read her mind about returning to the town. "I loved coming here to visit my grandparents." She exhaled heavily and looked into the cloudy sky. "I loved the Magleby Mansion. I still do. So when I started my construction firm, I knew I wanted to work in a small town."

Trent looked at her out of the side of his eyes. "Wouldn't that make things harder?"

"Yeah, it's not the easiest," she said. "But I like working on smaller projects where I get to know people. I'm not interested in being a homebuilder, cranking out cookie cutter buildings and all that."

"So, like, my deck isn't beneath you."

"Are you kidding?" She looked fully at him, and Trent Baker didn't seem like the kidding kind. "Your deck is a dream project," she said with a smile and absolute sincerity. "I can't wait to do it."

"Better than building tree stands, I guess." He grinned at her, and Lauren laughed.

"Definitely." Happiness soared through her, and she hoped Trent was having a good time. They had another couple of blocks until they reached The Anchor, which sat across the street from the town square.

"So, what about you?" she asked. "Porter is how old?"

"Six. He's in first grade."

"Siblings?" Maybe if Lauren didn't think about what it would be like to have a six-year-old she had to take care of, she could ignore her trepidation over the subject.

"Just an older sister," he said. "Eliza. She's married and has two girls."

"And she lives here."

"In Hawthorne Harbor, yes. My parents still live in Bell Hill."

"I've done some work up there," she said. "It's a beautiful town."

"Yes, it is." Trent kept walking, the silence between them just a touch awkward. "Guess I should've dropped this in my truck," he said with a nervous chuckle.

"You weren't going to present it to me over soup?"

Their eyes met and the electricity between them sent shock waves into the atmosphere. If Kam had been there, he'd be shouting about a live wire and to cut the power.

But Lauren didn't want to cut this connection between them. "I asked you out in March," she said. "I had no idea who you were, or that your wife had just died, or that you had a son." Why she was telling him any of this, she didn't know. But she couldn't stop herself now. "It was no big deal. I felt like an idiot when I found out. But I'm glad we're going out now."

There, she'd said it.

"Me too," he said simply. But he said so much more when he shifted the folder to his other hand and reached for hers. Her whole body sighed as she aligned her fingers between his, and it felt like even the clouds approved of this first date, as they moved aside and let the sun shine down on Lauren and Trent.

"So clam chowder, huh?" he asked.

"It's my favorite," she said. "Do you like seafood?"

"Not particularly."

"But you grew up on the coast." She looked at him, genuinely wanting to know what made him tick.

"Is that a rule?" he asked playfully. "You grow up near the ocean and you have to like seafood?"

Lauren laughed and shook her head. "You win. I grew up in the technology capital of the US, and I barely know how to use my phone."

Trent chuckled and tightened his grip on her fingers. "Um, I don't want to alarm you, but that's my sister."

Lauren's gaze flew down the sidewalk to where a group of four women stood. They had formed a huddle, their chatter reaching Lauren's ears from a hundred yards away.

"And this?" She lifted their still-joined hands. "Is this a problem?"

Trent tugged her a little closer. "Not for me. Eliza

knows I've been dating." But there was something aloof in his tone, something he was hiding.

Sure enough, when he said, "Hey, Eliza," and his sister turned toward them, pure surprise flowed over her fair features as she took in Lauren and the way Trent had a hold of her hand.

"Trent, what are you doing out?"

He rolled his eyes. "I get out, you know."

"Only with the dogs." Eliza glanced at Lauren. "I'm Eliza, Trent's sister."

"Yes," Lauren said, smiling. "He was just telling me about you." The weight of the other three women's eyes on Lauren felt suffocating, but she managed to keep breathing.

"It's our first date," Trent said. "I'll call you later, okay, Lize?"

"Oh, of course. Yes. Later."

Trent kept walking, calm and cool and without a hitch in his step. Lauren felt like someone had cut her off at the knees and sewn on new feet.

"How are you so nonplussed?" she asked him.

"I told you all of my dates have been a disaster." He looked down at her and smiled. "That was a minor speed bump. We're still holding hands and still on our way to eat."

"And I don't have a boyfriend."

Trent tipped his head back and laughed. "Right. That's

a big one, in case you didn't know. I had no idea I needed to ask that before I went out with someone."

"Trust me, I get it." Lauren waited for him to open the door to The Anchor. Inside, the atmosphere was vibrant and fun, with pictures of boats and crabs and anchors on the walls. The line was only a few people long, and she joined it, thrilled when Trent pressed in close to her as someone squeezed by to get to their table.

They talked about the town, his childhood, and her family, but they didn't circle back to his wife or why she understood that certain questions needed to be asked before dates could happen.

Lauren didn't mind. She didn't need to know everything on the first date. What she did know was that her instincts about this man from nearly four years ago were right. She was still attracted to him and she did like him.

"So," she asked after they'd eaten—he'd ordered a pastrami sandwich on rye and three bags of potato chips. That had sparked a whole conversation about the kettle-cooked chips and if they were better than their thinner cousins. He said no. She said yes.

"So what?" he asked, capturing her hand as they walked back to the community center.

"Was this a disaster?" She watched him, knowing the answer when he smiled.

"I think it was the best first date I've been on in a long time." He turned his grin in her direction and warmth filled Lauren from head to toe.

"Great. So we're on for Saturday night at the Mansion?"

"Definitely." He glanced over his shoulder. "I guess I really will have to call Eliza, won't I?"

"Were you lying?" She made a hugely fake gasping sound. "About calling your sister later?"

Trent laughed, the sound wonderful and magical, and Lauren had never been happier that she could infuse some measure of joy into this man's life.

"I wasn't going to call her and gossip about our date, no," he said.

"Good news," Lauren said, the sight of her construction truck reminding her how much she still needed to accomplish that day. "But maybe you'll call *me* later?"

Their eyes met again, and Trent ducked his head. "I'm not all that great on the phone."

A pinch zinged in Lauren's stomach. "Oh, all right. We'll text about the weekend then."

A frown crossed Trent's face, but he nodded. They arrived at her truck, and she fiddled with her keys, trying to figure out how to end this date without ruining it.

She hadn't been on a first date in longer than he'd had a good one. Lauren wondered what he'd think of that, but she kept it to herself.

"Thank you for lunch," she said, extracting her hand from his. She reached up and let it drift down the side of his face. He seemed frozen, so Lauren stretched up and kissed his cheek. "I'll talk to you later."

She spun and got in her truck, somehow managed to jam the key in the ignition and twist it, and flip the gearshift into drive.

She wasn't sure how she got to the Mansion, if any of the lights had been green as she'd gone through them. All she knew was that she really wanted to keep seeing Trent Baker, and that meant she had to tell him about a few of her biggest secrets.

7

T rent sat at his desk, basking in the good-date afterglow. He had no idea dating could be *fun*. At least he'd forgotten such things.

"Hey." Jason knocked a few times on Trent's desk. "Earth to Trent."

Trent looked up as if in slow motion. "Yeah?"

"I've been talking to you for five minutes." Jason looked around the station like anyone was there to witness his embarrassment.

"Sorry." Trent leaned forward. "What's up?"

"Kaitlyn says she's found your next date."

"Oh, no." Trent chuckled. "I'm not doing any more set-ups." That much was true, at least. He wasn't sure he really wanted to reveal his blooming relationship with Lauren quite yet, though he *would* have to talk to Eliza soon. He probably should've texted while he and Lauren waited to order.

In fact, he was surprised she hadn't called already.

"Come on," Jason said. "Kaitlyn wants to try Blue Wharf." He lifted his eyebrows as if to say the date would be worth it even if it was bad.

"You take her," Trent said. "I'm busy."

"With what?" Jason challenged, and Trent usually liked the sandy-haired lieutenant. They ran together sometimes, and Trent had trusted Jason with some of his most vulnerable moments when it came to women.

But no one knew about Kathy-with-the-boyfriend... except maybe Lauren. How she'd found out, Trent wasn't sure.

"My yard," Trent said. "I just hired someone to do the deck. No time for dating."

Jason snorted. "Yeah, I've heard that before." He straightened. "Well, are you at least coming to the Magleby Mansion unveiling?"

"Oh, yeah, sure."

"Kaitlyn said she has a couple of extra tickets for you and Porty. Unless you already have yours?" Jason looked like he'd rather sit with Trent than his own wife and two girls.

"You need tickets?" Trent didn't know that.

"They're free, but yeah." Jason cocked his head. "You better get them today. I heard they were almost gone."

"All right." Trent stood like he'd go get them right now. "Where do I get them?"

"All the businesses on Main Street got a stack, but Mabel has insisted that once they're gone, they're gone." Jason shrugged and added, "Let me know if you need some. Like I said, Kaitlyn got a couple of extra ones."

Trent lifted his hand in acknowledgement and wondered if he could leave work again to get the tickets. Instead, he pulled out his phone and texted Lauren.

That was a non-disaster. Thank you. He smiled at the words, thinking maybe he wasn't the worst dating single father on the planet. *Did you know we need tickets to the unveiling?*

Thanks! she sent back. *I had fun too.* A few seconds passed before she said *I have tickets for us.*

Us.

Trent liked the look of that word, and while he'd never imagined himself with anyone but Savannah, she'd been gone long enough that Trent had lived more of his adult life without her than with her.

Great, he sent to Lauren, and then he started thumbing out a message to his sister. *So I'm going to the unveiling on Saturday night with Lauren. Any chance you can babysit?*

Instead of answering in a text, his sister called. Trent felt like he was conducting secret mafia business when he lifted his phone to his ear, glanced around, and said, "Hey," in a whisper.

"Can you talk?"

"Yeah, it's okay." Sarah wasn't even at her desk, and Trent wasn't sure who he thought would overhear the conversation.

"So you and Lauren Michaels."

"You say that like it's impossible."

Eliza laughed. "Of course not. It's just...she's not who I pictured you with."

Trent took a few moments to think about it. "So she's different than Savannah."

"A *lot* different."

Trent frowned. Was he supposed to find someone just like Savannah?

"It doesn't matter," Eliza said. "You do you. But I can't babysit on Saturday. We're going to the unveiling too. It's why I was in town today with the girls."

Trent sat back in his chair. "I should probably bring Porter, right?"

"It's a big town celebration," Eliza said. "We could take him, if you wanted."

"And what? Have him see me dancing with Lauren? Holding her hand?"

"I've told you, you should talk to him about dating."

"He's six."

"Doesn't mean he's blind, or that he doesn't know what you're doing when you drop him off here."

Trent didn't want to get into this old discussion. Already, the high from completing a non-disastrous first date was wearing off.

"I wonder what Mom and Dad are doing," he said, thinking it next to impossible to find a babysitter in town who wouldn't be going to the unveiling.

"They're coming with us," Eliza said. "If you'll remember right, I invited you too. But I guess Lauren's invitation holds more weight."

"It's not that," Trent said. "She's the general contractor on the job, and she needs someone at her side for all the pictures."

"Mm hm. So that's why you were holding her hand on Main Street today. Four full days before the event."

Trent half sighed and half laughed. "I guess I won't be able to go."

"Sure you can. Talk to Porter."

"Eliza—"

"Gotta go. Thanks for calling." She hung up before Trent could tell her that *she* had called *him*. Didn't matter. He'd never succeeded at changing his older sister's mind about anything.

"Tell Porter," he grumbled to himself. He hadn't spent much time talking about his son during lunch. He'd learned quickly that women liked the idea of him having a son, but they didn't want to spend a lot of time learning about him.

He sat at his desk, his mind whirring. He got up and went out to the training yard, going through the motions of the easier tricks with Pecarino and Brutus.

By the end of the afternoon, Trent could see two

choices. Ask Lauren if she had a ticket for Porter too and find out if she was okay with him coming. Or back out and not go at all.

He pulled out his phone to send another text, thought better of it, and dialed her instead.

"Hey," she said, surprise evident in her voice. "You said you wouldn't call."

"No," he said. "I said I was bad on the phone." He cleared his throat, the breeze drifting across his face not nearly stiff enough. "I have a problem for this weekend."

"A problem? Just a sec." The background noise around her dulled, indicating she'd moved. "All right. I can hear now. What problem?"

"Porter." Trent squeezed his eyes shut. "I mean, obviously my son is not a problem. It's just that Eliza and my parents are going to the unveiling. I think the whole town will be there. I don't have anyone to watch him."

Trent opened his eyes, not encouraged when Lauren didn't immediately say, "Oh, bring him. He'll love it."

"So I can either bring him with me, or I can't come."

As the silence stretched, Trent once again had the distinct feeling that dating shouldn't be so darn difficult.

"Well, I want you to come," she said slowly, her voice low and echoing the slightest bit. "So I'll be honest, and then you can decide with all the facts on the table."

"Okay." Trent's stomach writhed. He didn't like the seriousness in her voice, especially when he could still feel the ghost of her lips against his cheek.

"I'm...not great with kids." She gave a light laugh that felt like it weighed two tons. "I don't like them. They don't like me. I've never wanted any of my own."

Trent had no idea how to respond. She really was one-hundred-percent different than Savannah, who had wanted to start their family on their honeymoon.

"Oh," he finally said. "I—can I think about that for a minute?"

"Take all the time you need," she said. "I can probably get Lyle to come stand by me at the party."

"Lyle Henderson?"

"Yeah, he does all my cabinetry if the job requires it. We're friends."

Trent had not heard her mention a single female friend, and as the thought rolled through his mind, he didn't know where to put it.

He simply had too many other things to deal with at the moment. "So I'll call you back in a bit," he said. "All right?"

"All right." She sounded like they'd been discussing which color of stain he'd like for his deck, not the entire future of their relationship.

Trent slipped his phone back in his pocket, his brain whirring through what she'd said.

"This doesn't have to be this big of a thing," he told himself and the four German shepherds still running around the yard. "It's a party. She's going to have to meet Porter eventually."

Indecision raged in him. Maybe she'd told him about her dislike of children, hoping he'd break up with her. Were they even dating? Did one date count as dating?

If so, he'd dated a lot of people recently.

He didn't want his sister to be right, but maybe, just this once, she was.

Trent suddenly needed to get home so he could talk to Porter, work things out, and then call Lauren again.

He did not want only one lunch with her; he wanted more. And that thought scared him as much as it drove him to have a hard conversation with a six-year-old.

8

Lauren couldn't focus, and she ended up trying to put the wrong light fixture in the room immediately through the door into the west wing.

Mabel had caught her just before she was about to launch her screwdriver into the painted plaster across the room.

"What's gotten you all worked up?" Her great aunt had a way of seeing things that Lauren tried to hide.

"Nothing." Lauren sheathed her screwdriver, Trent's words still bouncing around inside her brain. "Do you have any of those lemon bars left?"

A group of women had come through the Mansion the day before on their sister's trip, and Aunt Mabel had made lemon bars and coconut cream pie. But if Lauren knew anything about Mabel, it was that the leftover pie was long gone.

"Down at my house." Mabel eyed her for another moment, then switched her gaze to the innocent light fixture. "Come on. This can wait."

Lauren knew nothing could wait, not with the unveiling only a few days away. But she called to Gene that she'd be back soon and followed her great aunt toward the steps.

She steadied Mabel as they went downstairs, through the kitchens, and out a service entrance. A private path edged with ivy on both sides led to Mabel's home, which sat right on Mansion property.

Lauren felt like she'd swallowed a hurricane, but she didn't say anything. Thankfully, walking seemed to take all of Mabel's energy, and she didn't say anything until she'd entered her home and collapsed in the armchair.

"Lemon bars on the counter."

Lauren retrieved the whole container and joined her aunt back in the living room. She opened the lid and took out two bars before offering one to Mabel.

She shook her head, still trying to catch her breath. Lauren felt bad for making her come all the way back down here. She'd probably just gotten up to the mansion when she'd witnessed the light fixture abuse.

Lauren kept both lemon bars for herself, completely polishing them off before Mabel said, "Something's wrong."

Of course something was wrong. She'd told Trent she didn't like kids—and he had a kid.

And now she probably wouldn't fit in her dress too. *Not that it matters*, she thought. She didn't have anybody to wear it for.

"It's a stupid thing," Lauren said. "I'll figure it out. But I thought I had a date for the unveiling, and it turns out I might not."

"Might not?" Mabel reached for a glass of water on the table beside her. Her reading glasses sat there, as did a couple of mint wrappers.

"He's thinking about it." Lauren tried to keep the sarcasm out of her voice. "I guess he can't find a babysitter for his son."

Only a heartbeat passed before Mabel said, "Trent Baker?"

"Yes." Lauren saw no point in denying it. Plenty of people had seen them walking hand-in-hand down Main Street.

"Porter's a nice boy," Mabel said like that would solve Lauren's problems.

"I don't like children, Aunt Mabel." Lauren leaned forward, so many regrets streaming through her mind, from phone conversations to lemon bars.

She looked up at her aunt, pure desperation pulling through her. "And I told him that. I *told* him I don't like kids."

Aunt Mabel simply stared at her. "Well, that wasn't very smart."

"Perhaps not." But wasn't it better to be forthright in

the beginning? She'd rather know now if she and Trent even had a chance than risk her heart all over again.

"And he doesn't know about Rick."

"No one needs to know about Rick," Aunt Mabel said. "Besides, there's plenty of time to talk about past relationships. Has he said much about his wife?"

"No."

"See? He won't care about Rick."

"Probably not." Lauren glanced at the lemon bars, really wanting a third. "But I don't even know if there will be a second date now that I've said I don't like children."

Mabel rocked back and forth in the armchair. "He and Savannah were married right here at the Mansion. I can remember it like it was yesterday." She wore a nostalgic smile, and Lauren decided she really didn't have time to take a trip down memory lane with her great aunt. Especially if the memories were going to be about Trent and his first wife.

He should get to tell her whatever he was comfortable sharing, and Lauren stood. "I have so much to get done still. Thanks for the lemon bars."

"Of course." Mabel didn't make a move to get up. "Tell Jaime to send my dinner down here, would you?"

"Sure thing." Lauren swept a kiss across Mabel's forehead and made the walk back up to the Mansion, hoping she hadn't messed things up with Trent quite yet.

She got the light fixtures installed properly, did the touch up painting on the baseboards in the whole space, and hung three mirrors before her back complained very loudly that she'd had a long day. And that she'd have another one tomorrow.

Trent still had not called, and it had definitely been longer than a few minutes.

So, feeling brave and bold and everything she currently wasn't, she called him.

"Hey, there," he said easily, like the last time they'd interacted was in the parking lot at the community center.

"Hey." She kept one hand on the steering wheel and both eyes on the road as she navigated toward the beach and not the town. "I'm wondering if you've had time to think about it."

"I have."

Lauren waited. "And?" she said when he remained quiet.

"I've talked to my son," he said. "And my sister, and we'll be there this weekend."

Relief rushed through her. "That's great."

"Eliza will take Porter while we do...whatever it is your great aunt needs you to do. But I've spoken with him about you. He asked if you'd show him how to build the deck." Trent chuckled, but it sounded strained along the edges.

Lauren pushed a laugh out too. "Okay, great. I'm sure I can show him how to build a deck. It's not all that hard."

"Mm, okay." Trent sounded like he didn't believe her.

Lauren pulled into the empty parking lot overlooking

the beach. She rolled the window down to get the scent of spray and salt. "So are we going to talk about what I said?"

"The part about you not liking kids?"

"Yeah, that part."

"Maybe you just haven't met the right ones."

Lauren sighed. "Maybe."

"Porter's awesome, and he's excited to meet you. Besides, I'm not ready to stop seeing you."

An instant smile sprang to Lauren's lips. "Is that right?"

"About right, yeah."

"Okay, so do I need to meet Porter early on Saturday?" Her nerves felt like someone had just tased them. "Or should I come over and meet him before? Or—"

She stopped talking when Trent started laughing. "Relax, Lauren. He's a six-year-old, not a trained assassin." Something banged on his end of the line. "I have to go check that. How about you bring over a pepperoni pizza tomorrow night? You'll be his favorite person then."

Crying came through the line, drowning out Lauren's "Okay," and Trent practically yelled, "Okay, see you tomorrow," before hanging up.

Lauren sat in her truck, listening to the waves but unable to see them. She had the distinct feeling she'd just gotten in way over her head with Trent and his son. But she had a date for Saturday night—and tomorrow—and she'd just keep swimming until her head broke the surface.

"Just like always," she told herself as she put her truck back on the road and headed home.

LAUREN ALMOST DROPPED THE PIZZA WHEN SHE WIPED HER free palm down the front of her pants—again.

The front door opened before she'd even touched one of the steps, and Trent filled the doorframe. The sight of him wearing jeans and a T-shirt with the word COP on it made her suck in a breath and hold it while she climbed up to the porch.

He took the pizza boxes from her with a smile. "You look nice."

She glanced down at herself to remember what she wore. And it wasn't nice. Her black work pants that had a lot of dust and paint specks on them, and a T-shirt that should've been washed last week.

"I didn't have time to change," she said. "The artist my aunt hired to do a few pieces showed up today, and she needed help with some installation. That put me way back on a few things, and yeah."

She stepped into his house, expecting it to be as immaculate as his lawn. But it so wasn't. Shoes lay by the front door, toys littered the floor, and there was some sort of...fluff everywhere.

"The dogs got new toys today," Trent said, stepping over everything. "They shred them to bits."

She followed him into the kitchen to find all four canines lined up, one of whom had a stuffed squirrel firmly clenched in his jaws.

"They're so cute."

"They are not." Trent put the pizza on the counter and stepped over to a hall that led further into the house. "Porter! Pizza's here."

Trent met her eye. "Nervous?"

"Absolutely."

"Me too." He licked his lips. "I've never introduced my son to a woman."

Before Lauren could respond, a dark-haired boy came barreling out of the hallway, a dinosaur clutched in his fist. "Did you get pepperoni?"

He didn't even seem to see her standing there, and Trent said, "Porter, remember how I said my friend was bringing the pizza?"

Lauren cringed internally. Friend? Was that what she was? She had no idea what six-year-olds could or could not understand, and she supposed that she wasn't Trent's girlfriend.

Yet.

Where that word had come from, she wasn't sure. But it was there inside her mind, and it wasn't going away. Even when the little boy turned his cute face toward her and said, "Oh, that's right. Did *you* get pepperoni pizza?"

"With extra cheese," Lauren said with a smile. "And your dad said you wanted to learn how to build a deck."

Porter's whole fact lit up, and he looked back and forth between Lauren and Trent. "Yeah, I do. Are we gonna do that tonight, too?"

Lauren laughed. "It takes a lot longer than one night to build a deck." She took the plate Trent handed to her. Impressed that he didn't use paper, she smiled at him. "But I brought a couple of things in my truck. We can go check them out after we eat."

Trent gave her a curious look, but she wasn't telling him what she'd brought.

She had worried more than she should've, because once they all had pizza slices on their plates, they sat at the bar and talked. Trent asked Porter about school, and Porter talked about his friends. Lauren mostly listened, and while it wasn't anything like any of the dates she'd ever gone on, she felt like she belonged. She learned little about Trent, other than he made his son finish what he took and clean up his own plate. He wouldn't give the dogs any pizza, even when they all laid down in synchronized fashion.

"They're working," Trent said when Lauren asked him how he could withhold a reward.

"They're always working," Porter said.

"Do you do that?" Lauren asked. "Work all the time for no reward?"

Trent looked at her coolly. "Yes."

Lauren laughed, glad when a smile cracked Trent's

stoic face too. "Come on," she said. "Let's go see what I brought before it gets too dark."

Porter ran ahead of them, and Trent let his fingers brush hers as they walked from the dining room, through the living room, and to the front door.

Her heart skipped, especially when he grabbed her hand and squeezed once before exiting the house.

Porter was already waiting down by her tailgate, jumping around like someone had poured ants down his pants.

"Back up, bud," Trent said when they arrived.

Lauren lowered the tailgate, realizing how messy the back of her truck was. She ignored it, just like Trent obviously ignored the buckets of fluff on his floors. "Okay, so this is called a window frame."

She pulled a box from under a tarp. "It's got four pieces of wood, and your job is to make the corners line up, everything nice and straight. See, that's what we do to build decks. All the boards have to line up straight. All the edges. Everything is flat and uniform."

Even as she spoke, Lauren felt the passion she had for taking gnarled wood and making it beautiful, or gutting a room and redoing it into something functional, infuse her voice.

She set the box on the ground, but it still came up to her knees. "This one's for kids. So it's got a child-sized hammer." She ripped open the top of the box and pulled out the tools. "And enough nails to try a few times." She handed the plastic bag with the hammer and nails to Porter, whose eyes were as big as the moon.

"This is for me?"

"Well, your dad can't use a child-size hammer." Lauren laughed and continued digging in the box until she found the instruction manual. "Once you get it all straight and lined up, you can paint it. Or stain it. Mine's on my front door, like a wreath."

Porter just blinked at her until she handed him the packet. He looked at the picture on the front. "And I get to build it."

"That's right," she said. "Your dad can help. Or I can." Where that last sentence had come from, Lauren had no idea, but she knew she'd done good by skipping her opportunity to change her clothes and instead, stopping by the hardware store for this kit.

Because Porter launched himself at her and wrapped his bony little arms around her waist, hugging her tight.

Lauren had no idea what to do, so she stared at Trent and patted his son's back.

Trent gaped back at her, a look of complete shock on his face.

9

Trent had no idea what was going on. Porter didn't hug anyone except for him. Trent had never paid much attention to it until that moment, with his son gripping Lauren like she'd saved his life.

"Evening, Trent."

He turned from the scene at the back of Lauren's truck to find Betsy Brown standing there.

"Oh, hey, Betsy." He spied a bag of French bread in her hand. "What is that?"

She laughed and shook her head. "As if you don't know." She passed the bread over to him, and it was still hot. "Chicken cheese bread. Right from the oven."

"Thank you so much." Trent didn't have the heart to tell her they'd already eaten. He hoped Porter would keep his mouth shut too. Betsy lived right next door, and she brought dinner over a couple of nights a week, with no rhyme or reason to the schedule.

"Betsy, this is our friend, Lauren."

She seemed relieved to be able to step away from Porter, and though the sun was rapidly setting, Trent caught a hint of redness in her face.

"Nice to meet you, Betsy." She shook the older woman's hand while Trent nudged Porter forward.

"Ma'am," the boy said, going right back to the window frame set.

"Betsy taught me everything I know about gardening," Trent said.

"Oh, I did not."

"She did," he insisted. "You should've seen this yard when I first moved in."

"His thumb's as green as they come. Why, just a month ago he saved one of my trees."

Lauren looked back and forth between them, and Trent finally acquiesced. "Fine. But when I have a question, I go straight to Betsy." He gave her a smile, and she accepted it.

"How's Philo?" he asked, which caused Betsy's face to fall. Trent really wanted to take half a step forward and claim Lauren's hand in his, but he didn't.

"It's a bad day," she said. "Hopefully tomorrow will be better."

"Hopefully," Trent said. "Thank you for the chicken cheese bread."

Betsy waved and started back toward her house. Trent took that half-step forward and leaned his mouth toward Lauren's ear. "Her husband had a stroke about a year ago."

Lauren shivered though it wasn't quite cold enough for that. "That's too bad." She turned toward the house. "Should we go in? It's getting chilly out here."

"Dad, can you carry the box?"

Trent startled toward Porter, wondering how much his son had just seen. Embarrassment crept through Trent, but he picked up the box and started toward the front door with everyone else.

"I'm intrigued," Lauren said. "What is chicken cheese bread?"

"It's the best food on the planet," Porter said. "Well, besides pepperoni pizza." He happily went in the house, and Trent heard a distinct knock.

"Porter," he called. "Don't bang that hammer on the walls." If he had to fix holes in his plaster....

"Thanks for that," he muttered to Lauren as they went up the steps together. "If he breaks something, you're coming to fix it for free."

He was joking, and Lauren's laughter filled the porch, the entryway, the very sky.

Trent laughed with her, pulled her against his side before they went in the house, and pressed his lips to her temple. There one moment, gone the next.

She sobered quickly, but once Trent unwrapped the

chicken cheese bread, she brought back the sparkly personality and the quick wit.

Trent really liked spending time with her, and she'd played her cards perfectly right for someone who said they didn't like kids.

From what he could tell, she liked them just fine. And Porter obviously liked her. After the date ended and Lauren left, Trent took his dogs outside before bed. He stood beneath the stars and thought about his late wife.

"I still love you," he said to the brightest star, imagining it to be Savannah. "But I sure do like Lauren Michaels."

And he could find room in his heart to love again... couldn't he?

TRENT PULLED ON THE SLEEVES OF HIS JACKET, THE LITTLE American flag cufflinks perfectly in place. He'd gone next door for a haircut earlier that morning, and as he settled his hat on his head, he thought he looked good enough to be on Lauren's arm. He hoped.

Because he knew she wouldn't be wearing jeans and a tank top tonight. His mouth felt like he'd stuffed cotton in it. He was about to take a huge leap outside his comfort zone, and he hoped he didn't regret it.

"You almost ready?" he said to Porter as the boy came into Trent's bedroom. Water dripped from the ends of his hair, and Trent turned from the mirror. "A little too much water there, bud." He chuckled as he helped his son clean up and comb his hair.

He wore a navy blue suit Trent's mother had bought him for church. Porter had only worn it once or twice, so it still looked really new.

"Remember, I'm going to be a bit busy with Lauren sometimes. Aunt Eliza said you could sit by them."

"I know," Porter said, tucking his hand into Trent's. He'd been nailing and un-nailing the window frame every day after school since Lauren had brought it over, and Trent was glad his son had found something that interested him.

"Be polite," he said as they gave each dog a dental treat. "Say thank you. Don't wipe your hands on your clothes."

Porter didn't even appear to be listening, so Trent stopped talking. He was just nervous anyway. Porter acted just fine in public, and there'd be so many people there tonight, it wouldn't matter if he didn't.

So many people. The thought made Trent's fingers clench as he drove toward the Mansion. Lauren said she'd meet them there, and Trent sure hoped so, because he didn't even have tickets.

The parking situation was terrible, and Trent ended up parking down the hill because one of his fellow officers told him he had to. "The Mansion lots are full," Lou said. "Park here. Shuttle will take you up." He grinned at

Trent and said, "You're lucky you're not working this thing."

But Trent didn't feel lucky. Everyone would be looking at him. Everyone would see him and Lauren. Everyone would know about the soft feelings he held for her in his heart, though they'd just barely started spending time together.

He climbed onto the shuttle the town used for Beach Day and kept hold of his son as the bus rumbled up the cliffs to the Mansion.

The same glow that had caught his attention a few weeks ago emanated from the Mansion. People were pouring into the building, their faces cast in soft shadows from the yellow light.

Before the shuttle came to a stop, he pulled out his phone and texted Lauren that they'd arrived.

Changing at my aunt's. You can wait out front or come around the back. She lives down in the cottage at the bottom of the hill.

"Want to wait or walk?" he asked Porter as they disembarked.

"Walk where?" Porter looked up at him, confusion clear in his expression.

"Lauren has our tickets, and she's down at her aunt's house." Trent moved out of the way, already feeling the heaviness of eyes on him. He didn't like it. Not one little bit.

"Hello, Officer Baker."

Trent turned to find Porter's first grade teacher standing there, alone. "Oh, hi, Miss Terry."

She looked at him with stars in her eyes, and Trent had seen this look before. Not for a while, sure, but he could tell an interested female when he saw one.

"And how are you, Porter?" She looked down at the boy.

"Just fine, ma'am." He glanced at Trent, who grinned. "There's Aunt Eliza, Dad. Can I just go in with her?"

Trent turned again and saw Eliza and her family coming toward them. She wore a purple dress, as did both of her girls. Her husband wore a purple tie, and Trent smiled at the way they all matched

"I don't know if you can go with them, bud," Trent said as her sister arrived. "Your tie is blue."

"Very funny," Eliza said with a smile. She kissed Trent on the cheek and whispered, "Where's Lauren?"

"Coming." He straightened and said, "Porter's dying to go in. You have an extra ticket for him?"

"Sure thing." Eliza took her nephew by the hand and they marched right on by Trent. It was in that moment that he realized they'd left him alone with Miss Terry.

"You're not going in?" she asked.

"Oh, I am," he said. "My date has our tickets and she's not here yet."

Miss Terry's smile didn't hitch, but she started walking toward the door. "Have a good night, Officer."

He sighed as she went, not wanting to hurt her feelings. But going out with her when he had a girlfriend would be more hurtful, as he knew from personal experience. Plus, if things didn't work out with Lauren, he at least knew where he could get his next date.

But the idea of things not working out with Lauren made him cringe. She really was the first woman he'd been interested in from the very first moment he'd met her. And he'd asked her out himself instead of being set up. He really wanted things to keep going well between them.

He wandered away from the front doors, wanting a moment with Lauren where there weren't dozens of people watching them.

He took his hat off as he left the garden lights behind, almost wishing this night was already over.

Even with slow steps, he arrived at the back of the mansion before Lauren texted again. *I'm coming up.*

I'm at the back door, he sent.

A minute later, he caught sight of her making her way up the path. She stepped into the orange light, and Trent's breath stuck in his throat.

"You're beautiful," he said, staring at her. She wore a black dress that hugged and swelled and fell in all the right ways. Her hair had been swept up on top of her head, with the tail of a yellow ribbon draping over her shoulder.

"I don't even have the shoes on yet." She kicked off the

flip flops she'd been wearing and balanced as she put on a bright yellow pair of heels.

"Wow," Trent said, unable to articulate much more.

"Do I look like a bumblebee?"

Trent shook his head, gesturing for her to come closer. She did, but it seemed to take forever for her to take the few steps toward him.

"Are you sure?"

He took her into his arms for the first time as easily as if he'd done it countless times before. "No bumblebee."

"I feel like a freaking bumblebee. I shouldn't have let Gillian talk me into yellow heels."

"I didn't even know heels came in that color."

She giggled and pushed against his chest. "Come on. We're already late, and Aunt Mabel does not tolerate tardiness."

He grinned down at her, glad for these few stolen moments. "All right, beautiful. Let's go face your myriad of admirers."

She reached up and ran her hand down his face again, her eyes seeming to memorize things he didn't know he possessed. She inhaled, and when she exhaled, it was a bit shaky, the only indication of her nerves.

"All right," she said. "Let's do this."

10

Lauren felt one breath away from exploding. She drew in one more lungful of fresh air before committing to entering the Mansion. Trent's hand in hers made her feel like a real princess, because he was all dressed up like a dashing prince. If she'd thought he was handsome in jeans and a T-shirt, she was utterly drooling at him in his full uniform, complete with the hat.

The music inside the building was loud but classical, creating an ambiance that invited polite chatter and laughter, casual dancing, and light snacking on the hors d'oeuvres.

Lauren didn't take anything from the tray as it went past, as knotted as her stomach was. Trent bypassed the drinks and one-bites as well, and he instead steered her over to another cop.

"Lauren, this is a friend of mine, Jason Zimmerman."

"Oh, of course," she said. "You're Jennie's brother."

"He hates being introduced like that." Trent chuckled.

"Oh." Lauren felt like she'd been hit with a bucket of ice water. "It's just...Jennie is the artist we commissioned for the new wing. So I know her."

Lauren didn't know everyone in town, though with every job she did, she met more.

"Jennie's great," Jason said with a smile, clearly not annoyed as being introduced as Jennie's brother.

"Where's the family?" Trent asked, and Lauren inched just a little closer to him. Being held in the garden had felt wonderful, and she wanted to touch him, keep him close.

He glanced at her, clear questions in his eyes, and she slipped her arm through his as Jason looked around and said his family was here somewhere.

"There's Aunt Mabel," Lauren said, pointing toward the front of the ballroom. "I better go see if she needs anything."

Trent came with her, his hand as solid as cement in hers. Lauren tried not to pay attention to her walking, but she didn't spend a lot of time in heels, and it was much more difficult to navigate the uneven stone floor than she'd anticipated.

"Your seats are at the front table." Mabel pointed toward the table near the head table. "I'll introduce you at some point." She bustled off in the direction of the kitchen, her sparkly, silver outfit throwing glamour everywhere.

"Should we go sit down?" Trent asked.

"Yes." Lauren didn't want to stand and mingle, not if she had the option of sitting and doing the same thing. Only Gene and his wife sat at the front table when they arrived, and Lauren smoothed her skirt before she took her seat.

"You remember Gene," she said to Trent. "And his wife Sabrina."

"Nice to meet you." Trent shook their hands as Lauren contemplated how she'd introduce him.

"So are you two dating?" Sabrina asked as she lifted her glass of pink lemonade to her lips. She looked at Lauren, and it was obvious the question was innocent.

Trent looked at her too, and Lauren met his eye, trying to get an idea of how she should answer.

"Yes," she said with a giggle. "I think you could say we're dating." She glanced at Sabrina and volleyed her gaze back to Trent. "Right?"

He smiled, one of the biggest grins she'd seen him wear yet, and said, "Yes, we're dating." And with that, he lifted his arm around her shoulders and pulled her against his body.

The moment lasted for such a short time, but Lauren still felt cold when he dropped his arm and focused on pouring himself a glass of water.

Jennie arrived then, taking the seat next to Trent with a "Hey, guys." Bennett sat next to her, and while Lauren knew they were dating, it was still a relief to see their fingers intertwined. They both looked a bit nervous.

"Did Mabel tell you guys about the photographers?" she asked, and Bennett jerked his attention to her.

"Photographers?"

"She's called every magazine and newspaper within a hundred miles. She'll want us to talk about our pieces." Lauren gave him a sympathetic smile. "You'll be fine."

Bennett turned to Jennie and started having a hushed conversation about his pieces and what in the world he was supposed to say.

Lauren felt the same way. In her experience no one much cared about a general contractor. She wasn't an architect or anything, though a lot of what she did was envisioning a space and filling it purposefully. She was more like an interior designer who could nail stuff together and hang huge pieces of art.

Her right shoulder still ached from that tree Jennie had done. Beautiful as it was, it weighed a ton, and Lauren had to make sure it stayed stuck to the wall forever. After all, she couldn't have the thing toppling over on any of Great Aunt Mabel's brides.

Trent spoke to Bennett about his K9 dogs, and Lauren listened, wishing she knew more about police dogs and what they did. So she decided to ask, "And what are you training them to do?"

Trent focused his gorgeous eyes back on her, and as if Lauren wasn't already nervous enough. She cut a quick glance toward her great aunt, who wore a silver, glittery dress and spoke to someone Lauren didn't know.

She knew Aunt Mabel would be calling her up to the front, that the photographers hovering at the back of the ballroom would start snapping pictures, that she'd have to give interviews later. Lauren hoped she could string together coherent sentences that wouldn't be edited too much.

"I'm hoping they can become narcotics dogs," he said. "We don't see a lot of drugs up here, but they can go to other teams once they're certified."

"You'll send them away?" Lauren's eyebrows went up. She'd seen Trent with those dogs, and he obviously loved them.

"I'm training them to be working dogs," he said. "And we don't need four narcotics dogs in Hawthorne Harbor." He gave her a small smile. "The only reason Chief Herrin lets me train them is to get some recognition with the feds."

"Really?"

Before he could answer, Mabel made her way to the front banquet table and said, "Good evening." She wore a smile that could charm nations. "Welcome to Magleby Mansion. We'll eat first, do a short program, and then the west wing will be unveiled." She clapped her hands together, and everyone started applauding, Lauren included.

"Our local tradesmen and artisans who worked on the wing are seated to my left."

Lauren's heart gave a little hop, then a leap, as she stood and acknowledged the people clapping for her. She'd be called up after dinner was served, and she hoped every hair was in the proper place.

"You'll be able to meet them all in the west wing, where they'll talk about their creations and vision." She nodded toward the back of the room, and the wait staff came forward, plates of hot food already in their hands.

Lauren glanced at Trent and smiled, comforted when he reached under the table and squeezed her hand, a small grin on his face too. He was kind, and strong, and quiet, and Lauren really liked him.

Probably too much.

"Prime rib," Trent said. "Wow." He picked up his fork and knife. "Wilson would be so jealous."

Lauren couldn't help laughing as she picked up her silverware too.

"What?" Trent asked.

"You just said your dog would be jealous of your meal." She looked at him and giggled again, glad when he chuckled too.

A flush crawled up his neck and into his face, or maybe Lauren was just imagining it because the lighting was low and twinkly.

"I guess my life is a little tied up in the dogs," he said. "And Porter."

"I mean, I get it," she said. "I live, breathe, and eat construction." And sometimes the sawdust was a little bitter on her tongue, and it served to remind her that she didn't have a whole lot going on in her social life.

"Porter thinks you're made of gold," Trent said. "He's asking me to buy him a hammer. A real one." Trent shook his head, but his grin was wide and warm.

"I'm glad," Lauren said, still not quite sure how to relate to anyone if there weren't hammers and nails involved. She put a bite of steak and potatoes in her mouth, and groaned. "Aunt Mabel can never die."

Trent nodded, eating at twice the speed of Lauren. "What will happen when Mabel Magleby dies?" he asked.

Lauren took a roll and split it with her knife. "Uh, I'm going to inherit the Mansion." She cleared her throat.

That got Trent to stop eating. "You are?"

"I mean." Lauren shrugged and looked toward her great aunt. "She never married and has no children, and I'm the...." She wasn't sure what she was. Aunt Mabel had other relatives, probably ones better suited to run the most prestigious place to hold an event than Lauren was. But Mabel had asked Lauren if she'd run it, and she'd said she would.

"At least, that was the plan a few years ago," she said, looking back at Trent. "I'm not aware of a will change."

He leaned back in his chair, his plate practically empty, even of the green stuff. "And what are you going to do with the Magleby Mansion?" He grinned at her in such a way that she couldn't look away from his mouth.

"I have no idea, honestly." She half-laughed and half-scoffed. "I figured I'd hire a manager, someone who does what Mabel does so I can keep doing my construction business." She honestly hadn't thought about it, but she took another look at Aunt Mabel. It was clear the woman was getting up there in age, and she certainly wouldn't be around forever, even if she did joke that she would be.

Lauren had just finished her bread when Aunt Mabel stood again. She snatched up her napkin and wiped her mouth. "I'm almost up."

"Do I have to go up there with you?" Trent asked.

She shook her head, her eyes glued to her aunt. "No, but can you stay by me once we go upstairs?"

"Of course." He reached under the table and took her hand in his again.

"And now, I'd like to call up the brains and the muscle behind this job," Mabel said. "My great-niece Lauren Michaels."

She squeezed Trent's hand and stood, her smile hitched in place and feeling a bit plastic. Thankfully, she didn't wobble in her step as she went up front. The photographers *click, click, clicked*, and Lauren waved at the crowd.

Mabel glanced at Jaime, and the lights lowered until it was nearly pitch black in the ballroom. Then a projector brightened and a movie began. Lauren stood off to the side with Mabel's weathered hand on her arm to keep the older woman steady.

It started out with a trip up the stone steps to the west wing, each shot masterfully done, and Lauren leaned down to Mabel. "This is great. Who did you end up going with?"

"Stevenson's," Mabel said. The video continued through all the rooms in the wing, and then panned to Mabel who sat in one of the window seats.

"I wanted something better for my brides, though Magleby Mansion has always been the premier place to be married. And they deserve the best. So I hired the best." She smiled, that glowing, grandmotherly smile that made Lauren feel warm inside and out.

"And Lauren Michaels and her team have given every bride who comes to Magleby Mansion exactly what they deserve. Jennie Zimmerman has created masterful pieces. Bennett Patterson has graced the room with beautiful furniture. And so it is that I invite you all to go upstairs and enter the west wing. Take your time. Examine every piece. It's all waiting for you here at Magleby Mansion."

The video faded at the same rate the lights came up, and the crowd stood.

"Do you want to go first?" Lauren asked.

"No," Mabel said. "We go last, dear."

So Lauren stood with Mabel, glad when Trent walked up to them, and stood right at Lauren's side.

"You look so handsome, Officer Baker," Mabel said,

grinning up at him. "Just like my—" Her voice cut off, and a profound sense of sadness overshadowed her face. It only stayed for a moment, and then her charisma and smile returned.

Lauren glanced at Trent, who beamed down at Mabel. "Your who, Mabel?"

She reached up and patted her hair. "I had a beau once. A suitor. He wore the uniform, same as you."

Lauren's insides danced with this story she'd never heard. "Aunt Mabel," she said in a surprised tone. "Who was this *beau*?"

"It's our turn, dear." She started toward the few steps that led up the head table, and Lauren let Trent help her down them. He kept his arm linked through hers and escorted her out of the ballroom, his head bent as they continued to talk. It wasn't until they were yards in front of her, stepping onto the first stair that led to the second level that Lauren realized she was still standing there, mute and watching them.

She'd always liked Trent Baker, but watching him help her great aunt hit her right in the soft parts of her heart. Totally unfair.

She hurried after them, hoping she didn't twist an ankle in her haste. Arriving last in the west wing left her to face the reporters as a mob, and without Trent at her side.

"Miss Michaels," one asked. "How long does a job like this take someone with a business your size?"

"How big is your crew?"

Lauren looked past all the unfamiliar faces and found Gene. He startled and came over to join her, and in the next moment, Trent was there too. Lauren's nerves settled, and she took a deep breath.

"Well," she said. "Mabel Magleby hired us about six months ago, and planning began immediately. I work with a team of three as our core group, and we call in other tradesmen as needed. You'll see their work in here too, obviously, and you can talk to each of them."

She smiled as a camera clicked, as someone else asked another question. It was Trent, standing partially behind her, the light pressure he put on her back with his palm that kept her grounded as she answered.

11

Trent had liked Lauren before the dinner at Magleby Mansion. But to watch her conduct herself with grace and charm left his pulse bouncing around his chest like one of those rubber balls Porter liked to get out of the machines at the grocery store.

He kept his palm pressed to her back to steady himself, and as the interviews broke up and Lauren started gliding through the room, she affixed her hand in his, claiming him in front of everyone.

He liked it. So much more than he thought he would, and he tried to push back the biting guilt that suddenly chomped on his gut. Savannah would've loved an event like this, the robin's egg blue paint color on the wall, the intricacy of the sculptures, the mirror frame, the doors on the cabinetry.

She'd loved everything about design, and as he shadowed Lauren through the west wing, he realized that just because she installed curtain rods and hung drywall didn't mean she didn't see the same things Savannah had.

Lauren knew what each room needed, and how to install it. The tour took an agonizingly long time, and he was grateful Eliza had agreed to take Porter. The boy would've been bored to death, as Trent found his own attention waning in the second room.

Finally, everything was done, all the questions asked and answered, and Lauren turned to him. Her full lips distracted him, as did the way her fingers slipped up his jacket to his collar. "Having fun?"

"A little," he said, wishing the fabric of his uniform wasn't so thick. She looked tired and sleepy, but he couldn't help asking, "Want to take a walk around the grounds?"

She slipped her arm through his and pointed him toward the exit. "Sounds lovely."

Trent's nerves fired, but he managed to calm himself by the time they made it down the steps and outside. The night had cooled quite a bit, and he took a deep breath of the sea air as they paused on the front steps.

"The food was good," she said.

"It always is here," he agreed, glancing at her. "So, Lauren. Where do you live?" Maybe he should get some basics out of the way.

"Just down the hill actually. It's a little piece of property my family owns." She gave him a smile that nearly undid him and made him think about kissing her before the night was up. Could he do that? Would she think it inappropriate?

But she had said they were dating, and Trent had agreed. So holding hands with her felt natural, and he tried not to get too far inside his head. It was a strange maze in there, and he wanted to enjoy tonight.

"Do you like living in Hawthorne Harbor?" he asked, feeling like a moron. What kind of conversation was this? She was just so beautiful, and so poised, and Trent felt at least ten leagues below her. His gut tightened, and he wished he had his dogs with him so he could steal some of their comfort.

"You know what? I do," she said. "What about you? Do you like it here?"

Trent stepped, the lights from the Mansion dimming the further they walked. His eyes adjusted to the dark as he tried to find how he felt about being back in this town. "It's what's best for Porter," he finally said.

"Where'd you come from?"

"Seattle, funnily enough," he said. "I worked airport security there." And he'd loved it. Loved the hustle and bustle, the busyness of the people, seeing everyone's faces as they came and went.

"Savannah—that was my wife—she stayed home with Porter." Trent felt his throat tightening, the same way it always did when he spoke about his wife. He did it so rarely, and it felt strange to be saying her name to his new girlfriend.

"Sounds nice," she said, her voice almost a whisper.

"It was a good life." Trent took another deep breath, realizing he'd put a damper on an almost perfect evening. "But so is this one here. I like being closer to family, and yeah. This is a good life too. You know, if I had a deck in my back yard."

Lauren's laughter filled the night sky, the same way the stars did, and Trent sure liked the way it also infused his soul with light. He chuckled too and tugged her a bit closer to him.

"I think I can help you with that," she said, sighing. She paused at the top of the hill, the Mansion behind them. "That's my place, right down there. See the yellow lights?"

Trent peered into the darkness. "Yeah, I see it."

"It's nice living close to Aunt Mabel. She needs help sometimes." She gestured to their right. "She lives on the other side of the Mansion, down the hill a bit."

Trent turned toward her, feeling like they were the only two people left on the bluff at all. Though that wasn't true, as others had still been in the west wing when they'd left, it was a nice feeling. "I gotta admit, I'm wondering why you asked me out."

"You are, huh?" she asked playfully.

He just looked at her, kicking himself for letting his insecurity manifest itself. "I mean, you're...amazing, and I'm just a cop. With a kid. And you don't like kids."

Lauren's smile faded and she stepped back. "It sounds so much worse when you say it."

Trent sighed. "I'm sorry, I don't know what I'm doing." He gave a chuckle, but it was nervous. "Obviously, I haven't dated in a while, and I...feel way out of my league here." He ducked his head and started walking again. All of his muscles tightened when Lauren strolled next to him but didn't speak and didn't touch him.

They reached the other corner of the Mansion, and Trent thought he should just turn around, catch the shuttle back to his truck, and try not to mess up so badly next time he went out with a woman more than once.

"What would you say if I told you I was the one out of my league?" Lauren asked.

He looked at her, but she didn't meet his eye, instead just gazing down the hill toward the town. The lights winked back at them, and Trent's mind circled.

"Well," he said. "I'd say you were delusional and should probably go see a doctor."

Several long seconds passed, and then Lauren laughed again. Actually tipped her head back and laughed. "Trent." She sobered and stepped in front of him. "If you want to break up with me, just say it."

"I don't want to break up with you."

"Then let's get rid of the leagues, okay? I'm nothing special."

Trent reached up and ran his fingers lightly down the side of her face, every cell in his body sparking with energy. "Lauren, you're completely wrong about that." Their eyes met, and though it was mostly dark, with only the glow of lights from the windows and orange street lamps way down at the other corner, Trent could clearly see the desire in her eyes.

"We'll agree that we're both wrong then," she whispered, tipping up in those yellow heels. Trent didn't move, unsure of what to do. Well, intellectually, he knew what to do. He'd kissed women before.

But this moment, Trent wanted to memorize her face, breathe the scent of her skin, and take his time when he kissed her.

"Okay, we'll find him," a seasoned voice said, and someone came out the doors about fifteen feet from where they stood.

The sniffles and hiccups of a child crying came next, and Lauren turned to see who it was too. "Trent," she said. "It's Porter."

Trent realized it in the very moment she said his son's name, and he hurried toward his son. "Porter?" he asked, reaching him and Mabel in only a few strides. "Where's Aunt Eliza?"

"Daddy." Porter threw his arms around Trent's neck, and Trent picked him up.

"Where's Aunt Eliza?" he asked again, wondering if he'd missed a call or a text. He looked at Mabel, and in the next moment, Lauren arrived, her hand rubbing Porter's back.

"I found him crying," Mabel said. "He said he couldn't find his aunt, and I told him we'd come find you. I didn't think you'd left yet."

"No, we were just walking," Lauren said, and Porter reached for her.

Surprised, Trent slipped the boy from his arms to Lauren. He saw the shock on her face too, and then she got a good grip on him and patted his back. "It's okay, Porter," she said. "You found us."

Even Mabel was staring at Lauren like she'd sprouted horns. Trent snapped himself out of his stare-fest and pulled his phone out of his pocket. "Let me call my sister. She's probably freaking out too."

Sure enough, when Eliza answered, instead of hello, she said, "I can't find Porter."

"I've got him. Mabel found him, and they found us."

"Oh, thank goodness." She told her husband they'd found him, and then she said, "Where are you?"

"On the east side of the Mansion," he said, not really wanting to have this conversation right now. He didn't want to tell his sister—or anyone—that he'd been moments away from kissing Lauren. And if he'd acted faster, he probably would've gotten the deed done.

No one could ever say Trent had acted without thinking, that was for sure.

Fool, he thought as he reassured his sister that he'd

take Porter home with him. He hung up, and said, "Let me help you down the path, Mabel."

She hooked her arm through his, and he looked at Lauren. "You okay here for a minute?"

"Yes, go. Go." She graced him with a smile, and as she held his son, she was the most beautiful woman he'd ever seen.

He turned and walked with Mabel. "The party's over, huh?"

"It is for me," she said, back to her somewhat crotchety self. "I'm old, you know. I can't wear shoes like these for very long."

Trent chuckled and helped her down to the cottage at the end of the path. At the door, he said, "Well, it was a wonderful party. The Mansion is as beautiful as ever."

She paused and looked at him. "Your wedding was one of my favorites."

Trent's throat tightened, and he looked away. "Thank you," he said, unsure of what else to say.

"Do you think you'll ever get married again?" she asked.

"I don't know, Mabel. I honestly don't."

"Well, it's good to be cautious," she said. "Especially because of that beautiful boy up there." She reached for the doorknob and opened the front door. She stepped through and turned back. "But that woman up there, holding that son of yours? She's wanted to get married for as long as I can remember."

Trent blinked at her. "Really?" Lauren didn't seem like the type of woman who'd spent her childhood envisioning her wedding day.

"Don't break her heart, Trent."

"I—"

But Mabel turned around and walked inside, her sharp eyes the last thing Trent saw before the door swung closed. He stared at it for another couple of moments, wanting to complete his sentence.

"I don't think that's going to happen," he whispered to the wood. "If anything, she'll break mine." He looked up the hill, but Lauren and Porter couldn't be seen beyond the rise. He went back that way, very ready to be out of his uniform.

"Hey," he said when he got to the Mansion and found Lauren and Porter sitting on the steps. "We ready to go?"

"Yes." Lauren groaned as she stood up, and Trent hurried forward to offer his hand to her as she wobbled on those heels. She held his hand as she reached down and took them off. "Can you give me a ride home?"

"Of course. How'd you get here?" He reached for Porter's hand too. "Come on, bud. Time to go home." His son slipped his hand into Trent's, and they went into the Mansion as Lauren said she'd walked up to her aunt's to help her get ready.

They caught the shuttle, and Trent made sure everyone got up and in the truck before he followed Lauren's directions to get to her house.

It sat back off the road on a street where only a few other houses were located, and Trent liked the privacy of it. "Stay here, bud, okay?" He got out and walked with Lauren toward her front door.

"That was fun," he said.

"It was," she agreed. "Thanks for coming with me."

If she wouldn't smile at him like that, his pulse would stay at a normal rate, but there she was, gazing up at him with that gorgeous grin on her face.

"So we're okay?" he asked. "After my...confession?"

"I'm okay. Are you okay?"

"Yeah," Trent said, squeezing her hand. "I'll call you later?"

She nodded, reached for the knob, and slipped into the house like smoke through his fingers. He went back to the truck, the heaviness of single parenthood descending on him when Porter scooted over and pressed right into his side. "Can we get ice cream, Daddy?"

And Trent couldn't say no.

12

Lauren woke the next morning with the smell of Trent's cologne in her nose. The sound of his voice in her ears. *I feel way out of my league here.*

He was handsome in his uniform, and she loved his vulnerability too. "You're already in too deep with him," she told herself as she poured her morning coffee. It was clear he would be the one who decided how fast or slow they went, because she'd had a crush on him for years. A crush he hadn't even known about.

"He didn't even remember you asking him out." She sighed, added too much sugar to her caffeine, and went into the bathroom to pull her hair up. After all, just because it was Sunday didn't mean she didn't have work to do.

She went into her back yard, noting that it needed some attention before the icy winter rains came. *Next weekend,* she told herself. With the build finished at Magleby Mansion, Lauren could get back to keeping up with her own life.

Of course, there was the Festival of Trees, and she entered the wood shop determined to get twenty tree stands made that day. Every year, she thought she'd have enough, and she always ended up making dozens more at the last minute.

Not this year, she told herself as she got down the safety glasses and pulled out her tape measure. The numbers, the cuts, the hammering kept her mind from focusing too much on Trent. Every time she stood to straighten her back or change the radio station, she allowed herself a moment to picture his eyes as he gazed at her in the gardens last night.

He'd definitely wanted to kiss her. Had even moved to do it. She didn't have to imagine what it would be like to have him cradle her face—he'd done that too. When her fantasies started to run away from her, she pushed them away, exhaled, and got back to work.

By lunchtime, she had almost all twenty stands made and decided to call it a day. After all, she didn't have to work seven days a week.

The next day found her at Trent's while he wasn't there, measuring and calculating supplies. They texted a few times, all about business and what kind of wood and stain he wanted, and she went to the lumber yard and the hardware store and purchased everything she needed for the project.

Just standing in his yard made her heart pitter-patter in her chest, and when she heard the slam of a door and the bark of a dog, she knew she'd get to see the man she'd been thinking about for so long.

Porter arrived first, crashing through the gate with his backpack flailing on his back.

"Hey, Porter," she said, lowering her clipboard. She did like the boy, but she had no idea why he'd clung to her the way he had on Saturday. She'd never considered herself maternal in any way, and she'd never been all that nurturing, even to herself.

"Lauren," he said, panting. "We're having Career Day at school next week."

She smiled at him as he climbed the back steps and sat down. "That's great." She tried not to look for his dad, but she couldn't help herself.

Sure enough, Trent entered the back yard too, all four of his dogs flanking him. He spoke to them in a stern, quiet voice, and they sat. They watched her, but they listened to him. She still had supplies to check off and another load to bring in from her truck, but she couldn't move. After all, the dogs weren't moving yet.

Trent met her eye and smiled. "Hey," he said, starting toward her. One of the dogs whined, but he paused and shushed it. "You're still here."

"I have everything," she said. "Just unloading and checking everything off. Then I'll be out of your hair."

Something crossed his face, but Lauren couldn't place it. A frown maybe? "Need help?"

"Sure, there's more in the truck." All the lumber had been delivered from the yard, and she hadn't had to unload that. "Is the wood okay where it is?" She'd had them stack it beside the fence, away from any of his bushes and flowers but still within her reach.

He glanced at it, then his son, then her. "Yeah, it's fine."

"Great." She walked toward him, hoping the slight tremble of anticipation of touching him didn't show in her fingers or her step.

"Let me get Porter settled with a snack," he said as she approached. "And get these dogs out of my hair. Then I'll come help you."

"All right." She passed him, wondering what kind of game they were playing. Whatever it was, she liked it. He caught her fingers with his as she passed, a brief touch that was there one moment and gone the next.

"Can I pat the dogs?" she asked, pausing in front of them.

"Oh, all right," he said with a tease in his voice. He barked a command at them, and they all stood, their tails wagging.

Lauren laughed as she bent down to scrub them all down, one of them licking her arm and another barking in a playful way.

"Tornado," Trent admonished. "Quietly."

The dog didn't quiet, and Trent called them over to him, directing them into a kennel while Lauren watched him. He didn't even have to touch the dogs to get them to do what he wanted, and when he turned back, she ducked her head and hurried out of the yard.

She waited at her truck, checking the supplies there before taking them back, something she didn't usually do. But if she could watch Trent use his muscles to haul boxes of nails and cans of stain, she was going to.

He came out the front door several minutes later, an apology quickly following. "Apparently, we need more vanilla wafers." He rolled his eyes. "Porter can be picky sometimes."

"Well, vanilla wafers are delicious."

Trent chuckled as he arrived truckside, easily sweeping one arm around her and pulling her into an embrace. "It's good to see you."

"What'd you do yesterday?" she asked. They hadn't texted much, other than about his schedule for today and if she could get into the back yard when he wasn't home.

"Oh, took the dogs running on the beach. Took Porter to the drive-in over in Lakeside."

"Sounds fun," she said. "I haven't been to a drive-in movie in years. I didn't even know there was one around."

"It's about a thirty-minute drive to get there," he said, stepping back but keeping his hand on her waist. "We should go sometime."

She smiled up at him. "I'd like that."

He nodded and looked in the back of her truck. "Okay, so let's get this unloaded." They worked together, taking several trips and making easy conversation as they moved the rest of the supplies into the back yard. He closed the gate after the last load and caught her hand again.

"Thanks, Lauren," he said, bending down and sweeping his lips right across her forehead. "I'd ask you to stay for dinner, but I'm not cooking tonight, and I don't feel much like goin' out."

"Want me to run into town and grab something?" Did she sound too desperate to stay? She knew Porter liked pepperoni pizza and chicken cheese bread. She knew where to get one of those.

"If you want." Trent yawned. "But you don't have to. I'm tired. I won't be good company."

"Then the dogs will keep my company," she said. "I'll run down to Duality. It's five minutes away. What does Porter like there?"

"The mini tacos," he said, a smile brightening his handsome face and lighting his eyes from within.

"And you?" she asked.

"Surprise me."

Oh, that was dangerous, and Lauren's heartrate kicked up a notch. She left him standing by the gate and got in her truck, thinking about how Trent had liked the prime rib and mashed potatoes at the Mansion.

She kicked herself for being so resistant to listening to

Aunt Mabel talk about his first wedding. She could probably get a clue from that. No seafood, she knew that.

Before she knew it, she pulled into Duality and took the last spot. With everyone on their way home from work, she'd be lucky if there was any hot food left. But she did manage to get two boxes of mini tacos, as well as two of the tater tots—her favorite.

Trent had ordered a pastrami sandwich last week at The Anchor, and he liked the thin potato chips. She grabbed a couple of bags of those and wandered past the pizzeria. The barbecue chicken looked good, and she made a quick decision by grabbing it.

She loaded up with drinks and got herself back to Trent's immaculately landscaped house. Inside, she expected the toys, the shoes, and the dogs, and she got all three.

She also found Trent sitting at the table with Porter, both of them looking at a worksheet like it was written in Japanese. "Food," she said, gladly handing over the bag with the bottled drinks in them to Trent.

She laid everything out on the counter just as Porter said, "Done, Daddy," and he came over to Lauren. "Did you get the mini tacos?"

"Two boxes, bud." She smiled at him and handed him one. "How's the window frame coming?"

"Great. Wanna see it?"

"Sure I do." She took her box of tots with her and followed the boy down the hall to his bedroom. He showed her how he'd made all the corners fit together, and Lauren complimented him on a job well done.

Back in the kitchen, she found both Trent and the pizza gone, and she wandered into the living room where he'd settled. She sat beside him on the couch and he offered her a piece of pizza.

She took it and they ate, and while there weren't any earth-shattering secrets spilled, Lauren felt comfortable in his presence, his home, with his son and his dogs. And when he started breathing deeper, she got up, took the pizza box back into the kitchen, and helped Porter get into bed.

On her way out, she paused and gazed down at the most beautiful man she'd ever met, falling a little deeper in love with him while he slept. She leaned down and kissed the top of his head and then snuck quietly out the door.

"Hey, Mom," Lauren said when her mom answered.

"Lauren, how are you? How was the unveiling? We're sorry we couldn't make it. Your dad's not been feeling well."

The unveiling was a couple of weeks old now, and Lauren only had one more day to wait until the applications for the Festival of Trees would be delivered to her. She'd taken two more jobs, and they were interior remodels, thankfully, as the November weather started to worsen.

"It was great," she said, fiddling with a pencil on her countertop. "I called, because I have a question about...something."

"What is it?"

She'd been spending her days working on the kitchen remodel at the Wheeler farm, and her afternoons with Porter as she built Trent's deck. They shared almost every evening meal together, unless he had a meeting or she had to attend to Aunt Mabel.

"It's about...." Lauren couldn't get herself to say it.

"About what?" her mom asked. "Lauren, you're scaring me."

"It's fine," she said. "I'm fine. I've been seeing someone."

"Oh." No squeal of joy. No happiness. No surprise either. It was almost a defeated sound.

"He's a nice guy, Mom."

"That's what you said about Rick."

Lauren nodded, though they weren't in a face-to-face conversation. "I know."

"What's his name?"

"Trent Baker. He used to live in Seattle."

"Mm," her mom said, obviously not caring about his former residence.

"We're working together on the Festival of Trees. He has a six-year-old son."

"Lauren." Now her mom's voice held plenty of warning.

Lauren didn't need her mother's approval. Neither of her parents had been particularly supportive when she'd changed her major to construction management, but she'd done it anyway. It had taken a couple of years, but they'd come around, and they'd never stopped loving her.

But for this, she desperately *wanted* her mom to approve of her and Trent's growing relationship. Why, she wasn't sure. Probably because she'd made such a mess of the last serious relationship she'd been in.

"I haven't told him about Rick yet," she said.

"Are you changing for him?" her mom asked. "Because Lauren, he should love you for who you already are."

"I know that, Mom."

"I don't want to lose you again."

"You won't," she said. "He's a great guy, Mom. I swear. I'm...wondering if you guys might be able to come for Christmas. Aunt Mabel wants to do a family thing at the Mansion, and the Festival of Trees will be done by then, and winter is my slowest season." She spoke in a huge rush, glad Aunt Mabel had suggested hosting Christmas dinner at the Mansion.

It was almost like her great aunt knew what Lauren wanted—a safe way for Trent to meet her parents, and for her parents to meet him—and provided a way for it to happen. With all the other Magleby's there too, the pressure would be less than if Lauren had a dinner at her house and invited Trent, Porter, and her parents.

"I'll talk to Dad."

"And Darrel and Eldon and Byron. I want them to come too. Everyone is invited." While she'd told Trent that her mom had run away to Seattle to get married when she was only seventeen and that it was a scandal, what she hadn't told him was that her mom was often still excluded from big family events.

"Well, you call them and ask them," she said. "Darrel is nearly engaged, and they might be doing something with her family."

"Darrel is nearly engaged?" Lauren really needed to talk to her brothers more. None of them liked to talk on the phone, but they were glued to their devices and would definitely participate in a group text.

"He's been dating Kimmy for two years now. I sure hope they're almost engaged." Her mom didn't sound happy about that, but Lauren didn't press the issue. Darrel could date whomever he wanted, for however long he wanted.

"Okay, I'll get in touch with them," she said. "And please think about it? I'd love to have you guys here."

"I'll let you know soon." The conversation turned to her dad, and what he was suffering from this time. He had several chronic conditions, and Lauren thought her mother was a saint for how she nursed him back to health over and over again.

When she finally hung up, Lauren stared at her phone, hoping and praying her parents would come for Christmas.

She needed to prove to them—and herself—that she could find a decent guy, and she knew Trent was that man.

"Will they come?" Aunt Mabel asked as she entered the kitchen.

"Maybe." Lauren sighed and got up from the table in her great aunt's dining room. "Mom said she'd talk to Dad, and I'm going to text my brothers."

Aunt Mabel wore a look of sympathy, and she shuffled into the living room with Lauren behind her. "We all make mistakes, Lauren. You're a good woman, and they'll see it when they come."

"They know I'm good."

"No, what they know is that you tried to be exactly what Rick wanted you to be. You stayed with him when he was abusive. You became someone else. And that hurt them, even if they still loved you and respected your choices." Mabel picked up her knitting. "You should be glad you never married him."

"I *am* glad of that," Lauren said, her feelings inside knotting and tangling. The truth was, her tumultuous relationship with Rick *had* changed her, even though she'd let her dyed hair grow back out and taken control of her business again.

"Have you told Trent about him yet?"

"No," Lauren said, sighing as she reclined the couch

and put her feet up. "We haven't quite gotten to talking about past relationships yet. We haven't even kissed yet."

"Girl, it's been weeks since you started seeing him." Aunt Mabel wore a twinkle in her eye. "What are you waiting for?"

"Him," Lauren said. "I'm waiting for him."

13

Trent's gaze got drawn to the Michaels Construction truck as he strode toward the front doors of the community center. Trucks and trailers crammed into the drop-off lanes, but Lauren's was right up front, with both the driver's side and the passenger doors open. The back held more wood sticking out in odd angles than Trent had ever seen.

His pulse quickened at the thought of seeing Lauren. Though he saw her nearly every day and had for weeks, every time they could talk was a welcome experience. After his shift tonight, he was taking Porter to see his parents in Bell Hill, so he wouldn't get to see Lauren at dinner that night.

His mother was making turkey, mashed potatoes, and pumpkin pie, because he'd been invited to Mabel's for

Thanksgiving dinner and he'd accepted. The Chief would be there with his family, and his brother and his wife too.

Trent liked Adam and Janey, and Jess too, though he was quite a bit older than Porter. He liked Andrew and Gretchen, and their daughter Dixie. And he definitely knew he'd be fed well, and get to hold Lauren's hand, and if he hadn't kissed her by then, he might explode.

But he didn't exactly have a plan for that, and he'd been playing things by ear. She was gorgeous to him, and sweet to Porter, and about half the time, Trent fell asleep on the couch while she was there, only to wake sometime later to find his son tucked in bed and Lauren's truck gone.

He thanked her every time, knowing she worked long, physical hours the way he did. He'd tried to stay awake, but there was something so soothing and relaxing about having her snuggled into his side, the television on, and their breathing happening in tandem. It lulled him into this sense of peace and comfort he hadn't had in so long.

He entered the community center to the scent of cinnamon and pine trees, not the greatest combination in his mind. He glanced around for Lauren, but there were people everywhere. Some stood along the front windows, guarding boxes. More stood in a line that stretched toward a table in front of the big multi-purpose room. That was where the trees would be set up, and Trent skirted the people and headed for the table.

Mitch Magleby and his assistant Alecia manned it, along with three more people wearing community center nametags. It seemed like people were moving through the line and past the table at a steady clip. He caught sight of Shawn, and he turned toward him.

"Morning," he said, shaking the man's hand. "I'm here to do whatever you need, and I've got someone outside manning traffic and keeping things civil. We also have teams of officers rotating in and out all day long."

"That's great." He wore a smile but kept a keen eye on the people. "This is crazy."

"I heard there were a third more registrations this year over last." Trent turned and surveyed the crowd too. A couple of people looked his way, and he lifted his hand in greeting. "At least that's what Lauren said. Said she had to order more lumber for the stands."

"She told me that too." Shawn sighed and added, "You can go in and see how things are going in the showroom. I think we have enough eyes out here."

"Sounds good." Trent stepped away from the man, the showroom his prize destination anyway. Lauren would be in there, no doubt, setting up stands and trying to stay one ahead of the people coming in to start decorating their trees.

He slipped behind the table, said a quick hello to the people there, and proceeded into the showroom. This place was much less noisy and crowded, though he knew everyone out there would soon be in here. With helpers, family members, co-workers and all of their decorations and signs.

He paused and took a deep breath, reminding himself of how much he loved the Festival of Trees. He'd brought Porter every year since they'd been back in town, and once he'd even purchased one of the trees to help with juvenile diabetes.

See, every tree was sold at auction for charity, and the good causes were as varied as funeral funds for a family member or sending the proceeds to help with cancer research. Some were put up in memory of loved ones, but even those were sold and the money donated to the community center, library, or other city offices.

One year, the wife of the retired Fire Chief had done a tree in memory of her late husband, and all the money went to a barbecue in the man's honor. The police department had finally been invited to one of the firemen's dinners, and Trent could still taste the steak if he thought really hard about it.

The room stretched before him, and he wondered if they really could fit over two hundred trees in here. Not only that, but shops would fill the hall on the north side, with dolls, handmade crafts and quilts, cookies and candies, and fudge. Oh, the fudge. Trent's mouth watered just thinking about it.

"Excuse me," someone said, and Trent stepped to his right to avoid getting struck with the giant gingerbread house coming through the double-wide doors that had been flung open.

"Need a hand?" he asked, stepping back toward the

door to find two of the community center helpers holding it open.

"We got it," Brandon Thrush said, his voice strained. "Back wall, Mandie?"

"Yep, keep going straight." She continued to direct him toward the main walkway that led back to the gingerbread house displays, and Trent just watched. He'd loved the gingerbread houses the best when he was a boy, and he'd tried to make one himself when he was thirteen. It had been an epic failure, so he appreciated and understood the skill and craftsmanship that went into creating the castles and palaces and quaint cottages that people brought to the Festival.

As the place started to fill up, he walked through the displays, helping a couple as their stand started to tip and then whistling softly as he simply patrolled the activity. It wasn't a bad way to spend the day, though his stomach did start growling by ten-thirty.

He caught Lauren's eye once and headed her way, saying, "Can you break for lunch at all today?"

She exhaled and wiped her hair out of her face. "Maybe if you bring something back and we sneak into a back room."

He liked the idea of sneaking away with her. Anywhere with her, and he said, "I'll get us something on my break."

She nodded, stepped into his personal space and squeezed his fingers, then turned back to Gene and another man whose name Trent couldn't come up with at the moment. "All right, guys. Is this one ready?"

Trent walked away when he wanted to stay, circled around several more times, and then stepped out to the lobby again. The line didn't seem to be getting any shorter, and the parking lot wasn't clearing out at all. He found Lou and said, "I'm making a food run. You want to go inside for a bit?"

"Have you seen the lot?" Lou looked like he'd broken up a dozen fist fights already.

"We have to eat," Trent said. "We get a break."

"Call the Chief and have him send over more people." Lou held up his hand and blew his whistle. "You can't come down here." He waved both hands and pointed to the right. "Parking is up the hill." He turned back to Trent. "There's no way I can leave until I have a replacement."

"I'll call Adam," Trent said, pulling out his phone. "I'll bring you some food. We can escape to a back room to eat." He couldn't believe he'd just invited Lou to his private rendezvous with Lauren.

It's not a private rendezvous, he thought as he tapped on Adam's number and the line started ringing. "Hey, Chief," he said when Adam picked up. "We need at least two more men up here. Lou and I are ready for lunch."

"Jason and Gil should be there by now."

"Really?"

"I sent them at the time your plan said to," Adam said. "You haven't seen them?"

"It is pretty crazy up here," Trent admitted. "I see why they wanted police at the setup."

"I'll radio them," he said. "Hang on." The line went mute, and Trent kept walking toward his police cruiser. He wished he had his dogs with him. That would really keep people in line. They'd be coming to work the bag station once the Festival began, and he couldn't wait to see how Wilson did. If he did well, he might be ready to move onto a real working unit.

Adam came back on the line with, "They're stuck on Locust. Gonna turn on the siren and get there."

"Okay, thanks," Trent said. A moment later, he heard the police siren, and five minutes later, he'd given them directions for what to do inside. "I'm going for food," he said. "Have you guys eaten?"

Jason gazed around and then shook his head. "No, get me whatever you're having."

Trent got in their car and kept the siren going to get out of the parking lot and away from the fray. The line at the deli was no better, as it seemed every citizen of Hawthorne Harbor had decided today was the day to eat out for lunch. He finally made it back to the community center forty-five minutes after he'd left it, laden with sandwiches, chips, and drinks.

Inside, he found Mitch and asked where the command room was, and Alecia got up and led him to it. Only two people were inside, and they were busy setting up sound equipment and making sure the electrical breakers were equipped to handle the incoming surge of Christmas lights.

Trent put the food on the table and used his phone to let everyone know where he was and that he had their lunch. *Send in Lou first*, he sent. *Then you guys can come in after we're done.*

He also sent Lauren a text that said, *Food in the control room. I'm back here now.* Then he sat, not realizing how tired his legs were and how badly his feet ached until he wasn't using them. He opened the club with extra roast beef he'd gotten for himself and had taken one bite when the sound crew vacated the room.

The silence felt like a balm to Trent's weary soul, as did the sight of Lauren as she walked through the door. Trent jumped to his feet and wiped his mouth, still chewing. He swallowed and approached her with, "Hey, there you are," coming from his mouth.

She sighed into his embrace, and Trent wondered if he could kiss her right here, in this back room of the community center, with wires everywhere.

She clung to him for only a moment, and then she said, "I'm *starving*. Tell me you got a Cobb salad with the lemon poppy seed dressing.

Trent's heart warmed, and he stepped over to the table and produced exactly what she wanted. "I listen sometimes," he said.

She flashed him a grateful smile and started digging in the bag. "No forks?"

"Uh...." Trent opened the second bag and pulled out the sandwiches for his men. "I got all of you food. Are Gene and...who else is with you?"

"Kam," she said.

"Are they going to come eat?"

"They're talking to Mitch real quick," she said.

"I guess they didn't give us any forks," Trent said.

"At least I know you're not perfect," she joked with a quick giggle, and Trent smiled at her.

"I'll go find you one." The minutes he had to spend alone with her were already tiny, and now he had to run out and find a fork. He cursed himself for not checking the bag and hurried into the hall. Thankfully, he'd been to the community center many times when they served dinner, and he knew where the kitchen was. When he returned to the command room, Lauren had found her soda and drained half of it and started picking at the lettuce in her salad. All the eggs were gone, and he handed her the fork so she could eat the rest.

"Thanks, sweetheart," she said, freezing immediately afterward.

Their eyes met, and Trent felt like someone had hollowed him out. He managed to sit down, never looking away from her, and said, "You're welcome."

She broke the connection between them, her face flaming red, and reached for her dressing. As she poured it over the salad, she said, "I get you want to go slow. I do."

Do I? he thought. He'd been thinking about kissing

Lauren for weeks, since that first night at the unveiling. But he hadn't done it. The time had never felt right, with Porter there, or him half asleep or her working on the deck in the back yard.

"But I have to admit something." She glanced up at him, and he appreciated that she didn't play too many games with his heart. "I'm tired of telling Aunt Mabel we haven't kissed yet. At this point, I'm not even sure she believes me."

He had no idea what to say. "Sorry," he mumbled.

"Maybe if you told me more about your wife," she said. "Maybe you'd feel more comfortable—"

"I'm comfortable with you," he said.

"Yeah," she said, stirring and stirring. "I know you are." Her voice strayed up into a higher pitch as she tried to be more casual than she probably felt. "But I don't think you're comfortable with *us*. At least not enough to do more than hold my hand and cuddle with me on your couch." She blinked and added in a rush, "Which is fine. I'm fine with it. I am."

But she obviously wasn't. "Maybe we should go out," he said. "Just the two of us, where you're not eating frozen pizza I made for my son, or my son isn't helping you build my deck."

A smile spread across her face. "Really?"

And Trent realized that he'd been stalling them all this time by letting her work in his back yard until quitting time and then hanging out with her there. "Yeah," he said.

"I'm going to visit my parents tonight. I'll ask them when they can take Porter."

Lauren pushed her hair out of her eyes. "I'd like that." She took her ponytail out and let all of her hair down, running her fingers through it. Trent wanted to do the same, dreamt of doing it, but he kept his hands stubbornly in front of him.

"And we're still good to go to Mabel's on Thanksgiving?"

"Yes," he said, finally reaching for his sandwich so he had something to do with his hands. "You're sure I can't bring anything?"

"*I'm* not even bringing anything," she said. "Mabel insisted she'd cook for us." She forked up a bite of salad and put it in her mouth. A moment later, Gene and Kam came through the door, following closely by Lou. Trent made room for them at the table, being careful to keep himself next to Lauren.

After all, he wanted her close to him, especially now that he knew he'd messed up by not kissing her sooner.

"HEY, MOM," HE SAID WHEN HE OPENED THE DOOR. "IT'S okay if I let the dogs in the back?" They hadn't been worked much today, and they needed a wide open space to run.

"Of course, of course." His mom scooted to the edge of the couch and got up. "Where's Porty?"

"He's comin'," Trent said, holding the door open for his son, who was balancing two boxes in his child-sized arms.

"I brought puzzles," he announced, and Trent followed his son inside, deciding the dogs could wait a minute.

"Where is Dad?"

"He ran to store for whipped cream. I forgot to get it for the pie." She took the puzzles from Porter and said, "Come help me with the turkey, okay, bud?"

He happily went, and Trent returned to the truck to let the dogs out. He got them in the back yard and went inside where his mother had Porter buttering the tops of the rolls that looked like they'd just come out.

"Can you run down to the basement and get a jar of grape juice?" she asked him, and Porter hopped off the chair he'd been standing on.

As soon as he was gone, Trent's mother rounded on him. "You've seen the same woman for weeks. How's it going?"

"I don't know, Mom," Trent said, a sigh leaking out of his lips. He knew his time was limited before Porter returned, and he did want to get some advice. "I haven't even kissed her yet," he said in a low voice.

"Well, what's holding you back?" She stirred the

creamed corn and turned back to him. "And it better not be Savannah."

"Yeah, no, I don't know," Trent said, wiping his hands up his face and back down. "At first, I felt a little disloyal to her. But now, it's...I think I'm scared of starting something serious and not being able to finish it."

"And kissing her makes it serious."

"Yeah," he said.

"And you don't want to finish it?" She took the pot of corn off the stove and set it on the hot pad on the counter beside the mashed potatoes and turkey, stuffing and gravy.

Trent reached for a roll and pinched off a hot corner. "I... like her. I like her a lot. Porter likes her. She seems to like us."

"That's good." His mother pierced him with her deep brown eyes that were a couple of shades darker than his. "You better let her know you want to keep her around."

"I know," he said. "We talked about it today. I need your help with Porter. I need to go out with Lauren alone."

"You haven't been going out alone?" Her eyebrows went up and she moved toward him, softening with each step. "Son, we'll gladly take Porter anytime. You and Lauren, this could be something wonderful. Don't worry so much about it." She ran her fingers down the side of his face and cradled his jaw in her palm. "Remember with Savannah how you just knew she should be your wife? This can be like that if you'd get out of your own way."

"Yeah," he said, and the rumble of the garage door said

his dad had returned from the grocery store. Porter's puffing breaths said he was almost back to the top of the stairs with the juice.

So Trent let the conversation die there, but it went on in his head. He didn't want to argue with his mother, but no, this relationship with Lauren could never be like the one with Savannah. They were two totally different people, and he had more than himself to consider these days.

So maybe it was okay that he'd gone a little slower than he otherwise might have. Than he'd ever gone in the past. After all, Lauren hadn't left him.

Yet.

14

L auren saw Gillian shake her bangs out of her eyes and lift her phone to eye-level. She had a thing about not looking down at her phone, because she'd read an article about neck strain and cell phones.

Lauren waved when her best friend glanced up after reading the text. She smiled and cut a glance toward her boss, who was arranging flowers in a vase. Then she walked over to the woman and had a brief conversation before escaping out the front door to the sidewalk where Lauren waited.

"What did you tell her?"

"I have to bring back the seafood bisque," she said. "It's so dead right now anyway. No one is interested in buying a house during the holidays." Gillian stuck her hands in her jacket pockets and picked up the pace. "It's freezing out here."

With Thanksgiving only two days away and still no private date with Trent on the horizon, Lauren needed a girls' lunch to figure out what to do about him. She'd already briefed Gillian on the topic, and she expected a hundred questions.

Gillian waited until they had soups and salads and had found a booth in the corner of Soupers, the most popular place for female lunch dates during the week. "So," she said once she'd filled her soda and mixed the cheese into her chili. "No kissing yet?"

"No date yet," she said. "I don't want to pressure him."

"Maybe he's waiting for Thanksgiving. You know, make the holiday memorable."

"His son and all of his friends will be there," Lauren said. "So I don't think so."

"How does your great aunt know all of his friends?" Gillian asked, totally a question Lauren hadn't been expecting.

"Everyone knows Aunt Mabel," she said dismissively. "Everyone who gets married at the Mansion, at least."

"Hm." Gillian tossed her head, but her bangs stayed in her eyes. Why she wouldn't cut them, Lauren didn't know. "Okay, here's what you have to do, and I know you don't want to. But you like this man, right?"

Lauren could only nod, her garden chowder not nearly as delicious as she remembered. In fact, not much of anything tasted good these days. She was consumed with thoughts of Trent, and she barely ate as it was because she forgot. Because she was thinking about Trent.

"Then *you* have to kiss *him*," Gillian said. "No more waiting for him. No more hoping he plans this perfect romantic getaway. Just go over there tonight, and kiss him."

"Tonight?"

Gillian stared at Lauren until she felt uncomfortable. "Yes, tonight," she said slowly. "I mean, Lauren, what are you waiting for?"

She'd told Aunt Mabel she was waiting for him, but maybe Gillian was right.

"You sound like you don't want to kiss him," Gillian said, taking a big bite of her chili.

"I do."

"Your tone with *tonight?* was a bit freaked out. When else would be a better time?"

"I don't know," Lauren said, looking away. "Maybe that's why he hasn't kissed me. There's never been a good time." Or, and something she didn't want to admit or even think about, "Maybe there's no spark there anymore."

She looked at Gillian again, sadness seeping through her.

"Of course there is," she said with a wave of her spoon. "You guys are plenty sparky. Spark-tastic. Live wires. Just do it."

Lauren nodded and went back to her food, Gillian's

words reverberating through her mind for the rest of lunch, the rest of the day.

When Trent got home with Porter, Lauren was on her hands and knees on his deck, nailing boards in place.

"Be right back!" Porter yelled as he ran up the steps and across the finished part of the structure. "I have to go to the bathroom so bad!"

Lauren laughed and got up, her heartbeat flailing around inside her chest. Trent usually came into the back yard with the dogs a minute or two after Porter, but she wasn't sure she had that long for them to be Porter-free.

So she hopped off the deck and unstrapped her knee pads, striding toward the gate, where she almost collided with Trent and his four canines.

"Oh, hey," he said, stopping short so he wouldn't plow into her.

"Hey." She dropped her gaze to his mouth, put her hands on his shoulders, and lifted up on her toes. Her eyes drifted closed a mere moment before her mouth touched his, and fire licked its way through her core, her stomach, and up into her head.

Oh, yeah. There were definitely sparks flying. Infernos, actually.

Trent made a sound halfway between surprise and a moan, and Lauren pulled back. Before she could settle flat on her feet, he cradled her face and brought her lips back to his, this time kissing her like he meant to. Like he hadn't been taken by surprise. Like he wasn't standing in the shadows just around the corner from the back yard. Like he wanted to keep her in his life for a lot longer.

Everything inside Lauren melted, and she ran her fingers through his hair and down his shoulders before finally just holding onto him while he continued to kiss her.

"Hey," Porter said from around the corner. "Where'd you go?"

Lauren broke the kiss, but Trent didn't release her. "Go on," he said to the dogs, his voice throaty and low. The four dogs tore around the corner, and Lauren looked into Trent's dark, dreamy eyes. "That should buy us a few more seconds."

She felt giddy inside, and a giggle came out of her mouth just before he kissed her again.

"I REALLY DIDN'T MEAN FOR YOU TO HAVE TO GET A babysitter tonight," Lauren said a couple of hours later. Trent had his phone to his ear while he waited for his mother to talk. He shook his head and waved away her statement.

She'd spent an hour with Porter on the back deck, showing him how to nail boards and make sure the heads were flush in the wood. Then they'd cleaned up and Trent had said he and Lauren were going to go to dinner.

But finding a babysitter hadn't been as easy as he'd

thought. His sister wasn't available, and his neighbor really wanted to, but her husband wasn't doing well that night. Lauren had suggested they just take Porter with them, but Trent wasn't having it.

"Great," he said, turning back to her with his smile on full wattage. "We'll be over in a few." He hung up and leaned his hip into the kitchen counter. "They'll take him."

"Great." Lauren thought she should feel more relieved than she did. "He won't feel bad, will he?" She glanced over her shoulder to the hallway that led to Porter's room, but she didn't see him.

"Nah, he'll be fine. He'll have more fun at my mom's anyway." He came a few steps closer. "They'd like to meet you."

A chill struck Lauren right between the ribs. "Of course," she said evenly. "We're...that far along?"

He shrugged. "I don't know. There's no manual for when to take a woman home, is there?" He ran one hand up her arm and into her hair. Lauren fought back a shiver and smiled up at him. "Because if there is, I'd really like a copy." He grinned at her, and she felt like a schoolgirl with her first boyfriend.

"Are we going to talk about what happened in the yard?" she asked.

"Do we need to?" he asked.

She normally disliked it when someone answered a

question with a question, but this time, her annoyance stayed dormant. "I mean, I just sort of lunged at you. I just...." She let her voice trail off, not wanting to admit her complete obsession with kissing the man.

He chuckled as he planted his lips right against her forehead. "I don't think it was quite a lunge," he said. "And besides, I liked it." He ran his mouth down the side of her face, placing a kiss on her cheek, then beside her ear.

Lauren leaned into his touch, the feeling of electricity and lightning and tingling fire running through her whole body. When he kissed her, right there in his living room, Lauren was so glad she'd taken Gillian's advice.

"So we'll take Porter to my parents'," he whispered, bringing her close to his chest and swaying with her. "And you'll meet them. They're really fine people, Lauren. They'll like you."

"I hope so," she murmured.

"And then we'll go to dinner. Just us."

Lauren really liked the sound of this Tuesday night, and she nodded against his body. "All right. You'll get Porter?"

He stepped back and said, "Yep. And I'll come get you at your place."

She nodded and headed for the front door. For some reason, she felt like she was stealing him from his son, and she didn't like it. The drive from his house to hers took ten minutes, and she hoped Porter would be a little slower getting his shoes on or finding a jacket so she could run inside and change.

After all, she'd kissed the man wearing her work jeans and a T-shirt with a hole in the hem. Terribly unromantic. But this dinner would include something with a swishy skirt and shoes that didn't have any steel in them.

Twenty minutes later, Lauren pulled herself up and into Trent's pick-up truck with a, "Hey guys,"

"Hi, Lauren," Porter said, his hair combed and a blue windbreaker on.

"Heya," Trent said, flipping the truck into reverse. "Porter wants to know...well, you ask her, bud."

"Ask me what?" Lauren looked at Porter, and he seemed fine. Normal. Not upset that his dad was leaving him that night.

"I don't have school tomorrow," he said. "So I'm staying at my grandma's, and she said she'd help me make place cards for Thanksgiving dinner. Do you think Aunt Mabel will like that?"

Lauren looked over his head to Trent, who shrugged. "Let me call her and find out." She dug her phone out of her purse and called Aunt Mabel. She put in Porter's request, and smiled when her great aunt said sure.

"She says yes, bud. Do you have all the names of everyone who's coming?"

Porter looked stricken. "No." He glanced at his dad. "Dad?"

"Lauren will write them down for you," he said as easily as if he'd said the sky was blue.

"Oh, yes." Lauren once again dove for her purse, hoping she had something that wasn't stained or torn that she could write on. She found a receipt from the lumberyard from just yesterday and said, "Okay, there's me and your dad, obviously."

She put their names on the back of the receipt. "And Aunt Mabel. And Adam Herrin, and his wife, Janey. And their son, Jess." She wrote as she spoke.

"And Andrew," Trent said. "Remember you met him a couple of years ago at the Safety Fair?"

"Oh, yeah," Porter said. "He drives the ambulance."

"Well, he used to," Trent said. "He runs a lavender farm now. But he's coming. And his wife, Gretchen, and their daughter, Daisy."

Lauren wrote all the names in a list. "Anyone else?"

"I think that's it," Trent said. "Oh, wait. I think Adam and Andrew's parents are coming. Joel and Donna."

With them added to the list, Lauren handed it to Porter. "There you go, bud. I'm not sure how all those people are going to fit in Aunt Mabel's house, but the food will be good."

"Maybe she'll have the meal at the Mansion," Trent said.

"Maybe," Lauren said. "But I doubt it. She loves the Mansion, but she thinks families should celebrate in their homes." A warm feeling filled her then, and Lauren's excitement for this Thanksgiving meal returned.

A few minutes later, Trent pulled into the driveway of a white house with a huge porch. The railing had been painted dark blue to match the shutters, and everything looked perfect, pristine, and peaceful.

"Nice place," Lauren said when he opened her door and offered his hand to help her out of the truck. She straightened her skirt while he lifted his son into his arms. He got Porter settled on one side and took her hand with his free one.

"Make sure you tell my dad that," Trent said. "He takes great pride in the yard." He flashed Lauren a smile that felt nervous, and her own anxiety skyrocketed.

She licked her lips as they went up the steps, and the front door opened before they could knock. Trent's mother stood there, a wide smile on her face. "Hello, everyone," she said. "Come in, come in."

Trent set Porter down, which caused him to release Lauren's hand. She watched as Porter darted forward and wrapped his arms around his grandma. "Go say hi to Papa," she said. "He's putting a pizza in the oven."

The little boy skipped off, and Lauren stepped forward. "I'm Lauren Michaels. Nice to meet you, ma'am." She shook his mom's hand and fell back to Trent's side, where he swept his arm around her waist and kept her flush against him.

"Nice to meet you too," she said. "I'm Glenda. Wade's inside." She turned and led the way, and Lauren glanced at Trent.

He smiled and said, "Well, that wasn't so bad, right?"

Lauren didn't answer as she stepped partially in front of him to enter the house. Wade was indeed just closing the oven when they arrived in the kitchen.

"Wade," Glenda said. "This is Lauren, Trent's girlfriend."

"Hello," he said, his voice maybe a decibel or two too loud. He also wore a smile that seemed too big for his face. "I'm Wade."

"Nice to meet you." Lauren shook his hand too and glanced around the space. It hadn't been updated in a while, but it was functional. Practical, even. Well-kept. Clean. Felt like a place people lived, with stories trapped in the walls and secrets in the ceilings.

She wondered what she could learn about Trent from his parents, and she grinned at both of them. "I'm from Seattle. Have you guys always lived here in Bell Hill?"

"Oh, yes," Wade said. "Right here in this house for what? Forty-two years."

"Well, the yard is stunning," Lauren said, watching as Wade's face lit up. "I can see where Trent gets his green thumb from."

"Okay, time to go," Trent said, but when Lauren looked at him, he was smiling.

Glenda laughed and asked, "Would you like some coffee?"

"No, Mom," Trent said. "We're going to dinner, remember?"

"Oh, right. Right." She gestured them back toward the front door, and Lauren once again went first. "Well, you two have fun. So nice to meet you, Lauren."

"And you," she called over her shoulder. She couldn't turn back, because Trent's wide body was right there, keeping her moving forward. Once they were down the sidewalk and he'd opened her door, she asked, "Are we in a hurry?"

"Yes," he said with that playful twinkle in his eye. "And they're still standing on the porch, aren't they?"

She glanced over his shoulder and nodded. He rolled his eyes, turned around, and lifted his hand in a wave. He got behind the wheel, and Lauren stayed on her side of the cab though every cell in her body wanted her to scoot closer to Trent. It was as if his cells had strong magnets in them and were calling to her.

He backed out of the driveway and drove down the street. "She'd have us stay all night, you know."

"Would she?"

"My mom's a talker," he said.

"Oh, so you *didn't* get all of their qualities. Good to know." She laughed as she unbuckled her seatbelt and slid over on the seat the way she wanted.

He looked at her, then removed one hand from the

steering wheel and clasped it around hers. He came to a stop at the stop sign and glanced both ways. But he didn't go. He leaned down and she tipped her head back and he kissed her again.

And all Lauren could wonder was, *Why did I wait so long to do this?*

15

T rent's whole life had changed in a patch of shade just inside his back gate, about three hours ago. And now, he simply could not get enough of Lauren Michaels's lips. He kissed her and kissed her and still felt like he was starving.

"Maybe we should go to dinner," she whispered, but then she touched her mouth to his again.

He felt like he'd been transported back twenty years and every touch was a brand new experience. Every breath held such excitement.

Someone honked as they went around him, but he didn't care one bit. He was *kissing Lauren*, couldn't they see that?

"Or at least move off the road," she said, finally lowering her head so he couldn't keep kissing her.

"Yeah," he said stupidly. He'd been feeling a lot of

stupid lately, and he couldn't believe he'd waited so long to kiss Lauren that she'd practically lunged at him the moment he walked through the gate.

He got the truck moving again and set it back toward Hawthorne Harbor. "What do you feel like? Mexican? Burgers?"

She clutched his hand in both of hers and leaned her head against his bicep. "I don't care. You pick."

So he went to Eight Brothers, an upscale eatery that served salads with shrimp, and burgers, and pasta. It wouldn't be too terribly busy on a Tuesday night, as kids didn't eat free like they did in a lot of places around town, and they didn't serve tacos for Taco Tuesday.

"This okay?" he asked.

"Sure," she said. "I've never been here." She peered up at the surfboard above the doorway. "What do they have?"

"Great food," he said, opening the door to get out of the truck. She slid out after him, and he wanted to lean down and kiss her again. He did, but only a brief peck, something to show that he could kiss her whenever he wanted to now.

She laughed and pushed him playfully in the chest. "You're just going to do that all night, aren't you?"

"Probably." He couldn't contain the tremors running through his chest as he stepped onto the sidewalk and opened the door for her. He paused before opening the next set of doors. "Lauren, I'm...sorry about...the wait? Yeah." He looked at her, feeling foolish and brave at the same time. "I made you wait a long time for that, and I'm sorry."

"It's fine, Trent," she said, and he really liked hearing his name come out of her mouth. She reached for the door and asked, "Why is that, though? I mean, what was holding you back?"

Someone started to come through the door, and he edged out of the way so they could go by. Lauren went inside and Trent followed, trying to come up with an answer that wasn't his late wife's name.

Thankfully, the hostess grabbed two menus and said, "Follow me," so he didn't have time to answer. But he would, as soon as they sat down and were left alone.

Might as well be honest, he thought. After all, if he couldn't be honest with Lauren, what was the point?

"Your waiter will be right out," the hostess said, handing them each a menu. Trent took his, but he didn't look at it.

Once they were alone, he said, "Savannah. I mean, obviously not her, but yeah. Her."

Lauren met his eye, her menu forgotten too. "You must have loved her so much."

"I did," Trent said simply. "Losing her was the absolute hardest thing I've endured."

"How did she die?" Lauren reached across the table and put her hand over his.

He swallowed, wishing he had water already. He'd had no idea their conversation tonight would be so serious, but he knew it was one they needed to have. "Car accident," he said. "She was, uh, hit by a drunk driver on her way back into the city after a hair appointment."

The waiter arrived with two glasses of water, and Trent reached for his immediately. Lauren reacted slower and said they needed a few minutes to look at the menu while he gulped the cold liquid.

When they were alone again, she said, "I'm so sorry, Trent."

"It was only about four-thirty in the afternoon too," he said, as if that made it better. Or worse. Or something. "She wasn't out late or anything. Just some guy who'd been fired that day. Spent the whole afternoon in the bar." He shook his head, the familiar rage blossoming. He'd worked so hard to overcome it.

He unwrapped a straw and swirled it in the half-full glass of water. "It's...hard some days." He met her eye, hoping she could accept that it would always be hard for him on some days. And in that moment, he realized he was thinking about him and Lauren in the long-term.

"I'm sure it is." She darted her gaze away from him. "While we're talking about previous relationships, I've got something to tell you."

"Oh, yeah?" he asked, relief painting his insides—until he realized how keyed up she was. "Hey, you weren't married, right?"

She shook her head and pressed her lips together. "I was engaged, though."

"Oh." For some reason, Trent hadn't been expecting her to say that. She looked back at him, and he saw the absolute terror in her eyes. "Hey, it's okay," he said, reaching out to comfort her now. At least he hoped it was okay.

"His name was Rick, and he was not a nice guy."

Everything about Lauren was *so* nice, and he couldn't imagine her, a tough general contractor who worked with ninety-nine percent men, letting anyone bring her to this level of anxiety.

He rubbed his thumb over the back of her hand, the silence stretching between them. She glanced up and said, "The waiter's coming. Maybe we should look at our menus."

She slipped her hand away from Trent's to do so, and he let her retreat. His mind zigged and zagged through possible reasons a guy named Rick could make the beautiful, powerful, capable Lauren Michaels wither the way she just had.

"What's good here?" she asked the waiter, and Trent let them talk.

She ended up ordering the pasta carbonara with shrimp, and Trent handed the waiter his menu with the words, "I'll have the bacon cheeseburger with onion rings."

Once the man had gone again, he sipped from his water, and decided to push for more of this story. "And that's all? Rick wasn't a nice guy."

Lauren tucked her hair behind her ear, revealing a sparkly earring he hadn't seen. In fact, he realized now that her hair was down, and curled, and she wore makeup. Of course he'd noticed that she'd changed out of her deck-building clothes, but he may have overlooked a detail or two as he stressed about her meeting his parents.

"He changed me," she said, lifting her chin. "I would've done anything to please him, and I'd started anticipating how he'd react to certain situations."

"Like what?" Trent asked.

"He was emotionally and verbally abusive," she said. "Like, if we went to a concert and I wore heels that were too high, he'd call me trashy. Or if we went to meet his parents for dinner and I wore flats, he'd say I was lazy and looked like I didn't care if they liked me." She waved her hand. "Stuff like that."

Trent simply blinked at her, disbelief racing through him. "He said those things to you?"

"Constantly," she said. "So I'd keep extra shoes in my car and at the office. I used to be a secretary, did you know that?"

Trent shook his head, unable to even picture her behind a desk. She belonged with a hammer in her hands, a set of plans nearby, and the scent of freshly cut wood in her hair.

"Well, I did, because Rick said that was a job he could respect. None of this construction stuff." She reached for her water with a shaking hand, and Trent wanted to track down this Rick character and say a thing or two.

"How long were you with him?"

"Too long." Lauren set her glass down. "Years too long. My parents said they'd help me get away from him, but I was afraid." She smiled, but it was shaky and didn't belong on her face. "I was weak, and I lost my confidence for a long time."

"Lauren," Trent said. "You're one of the strongest women I know." He reached across the table and squeezed her hands.

"When I finally got up the courage to call off the wedding, he laughed at me. Said he would've never gone through with it anyway. That a woman like me doesn't get a man like him."

"He sounds like a real jerk."

Lauren gave a couple of barking laughs. "That he was." She looked at Trent, really looked at him. "And in that moment, I decided that I was going to do what I wanted with my life. I was going to be me, and I wasn't going to apologize for it."

"Good for you," he said, and he meant it.

"It took me a long time, but I'm starting to feel like I'm almost there."

"How long ago was this?"

"About six years ago, I guess."

Trent nodded, but a twinge of doubt squirreled through his stomach. He wasn't sure what to attribute it to, and he didn't want to ruin their first solo date in weeks. So he said, "I'm glad you didn't marry him," and she moved the conversation onto something else.

The food was fantastic, and the woman across from him gorgeous, and when they got back to her house, he walked her to her front door and kissed her.

"Best night ever," he whispered into her hair. "Thank you for that lunge in the yard."

She giggled and buried her face in his chest. He laughed with her, and Trent went home happier than he'd been in a long, long time.

When Trent arrived at Mabel's cottage on Thanksgiving Day, he felt completely inadequate with his measly offering of two pounds of butter. But that was what she'd asked him to bring, and he'd done it. The surrounding property smelled like sage and baking bread, roasted turkey and plenty of butter.

"Remember your manners," he said to Porter as they waited for someone to open the door. Lauren did, and she beamed at them.

"Happy Thanksgiving," she said.

He took her right into his arms, breathing deeply of her lavender-scented shampoo and all that good food. It seemed like he and Porter were the last to arrive, as he saw both Herrin brothers and their parents. "Are we late?"

"Not at all." She stood back. "Aunt Mabel just took the turkey out."

The Chief laughed, and Trent glanced that way as he stepped past Lauren and into the comfortable, albeit small, home. Somehow, though, Mabel had performed magic on the inside of the house, because a long table stretched in the dining room, almost wall to wall, with enough chairs for everyone to eat together.

He said hello to everyone, smiling and nodding as he made his way into the kitchen, where Mabel was clearly in command. "The butter," he said, setting it on the counter.

She looked at him, and it was the same soft, glowing look he'd gotten on his wedding day. His mind spun back to that time, almost eight years ago, and he blinked to get back to the present.

"Thank you, Officer," she said. "Now open it up and put two cubes on that plate."

He did as he was told, wondering when she'd decided to call him officer instead of his name. Didn't matter. Porter was off with the other kids, though they were twice his age, and from this vantage point in the kitchen, he could see everyone.

Gretchen wore a festive pumpkin-colored sweater and a pair of black jeans. Janey wore a dress with red, orange and yellow splashed all over it, like fall leaves, and kept one hand on her stomach as she talked, a small baby bump there. Again, Trent's memories and emotions rushed at him, reminding him of when Savannah had been carrying Porter.

Adam looked well, and as Trent had taken on the Festival of Trees, the Chief shouldn't be too stressed. Andrew seemed good too, and he and Adam chatted with their parents.

Lauren hovered on the fringes of Gretchen's and Janey's conversation, and she cast a quick glance at Trent. "Anything else?" he asked Mabel.

"You better go rescue her," she said. "She's much better with men than women."

Trent chuckled, but he'd had the same thought and it didn't sit particularly well in his gut. But he crossed the room and slipped his hand into hers with, "Hey, ladies. Happy Thanksgiving."

Janey's dark brown eyes locked onto his hand joined with Lauren, and then she reached up and hugged him. "So good to see you, Trent. You look great."

"Yeah?" He glanced down at his non-festive colored shirt. "This is blue. I obviously didn't get the memo about wearing an autumnal color."

All three women burst into laughter, and Gretchen said, "Autumnal. Excellent vocabulary, Trent." She leaned a little closer to him. "You should come in the shop." Her eyes darted to Lauren. "Get some *autumnal* flowers for your next date." She exchanged a glance with Janey, and they both grinned like jack-o-lanterns.

"I will," he said just as Jess came over.

"Officer Baker?"

"Yeah?"

"Do you still have those dogs?"

"Sure do." He grinned at Jess. "Your step-dad can take them home any night he wants."

"Oh, we do not want six dogs at our place," Janey said immediately, but not before Jess said, "Really? Okay, cool." She looked at her son. "Jess, no."

"I'll ask Adam." He hurried away as fast as he'd come, and Janey huffed.

"Thanks for that, Trent," she said, seemingly put out. "Adam will say yes. He can't tell Jess no."

Trent smiled and said, "Well, that's what dads do." He squeezed Lauren's hand. "Can I talk to you outside for a second?"

"Sure," she said, and he tugged her away from the other two women, away from the joyous festivities in the house, away from all the delicious smells.

"What's going on?" she asked as he brought the door closed behind him.

"Nothing," he said. "I just wanted to kiss you." He grinned at her, feeling a bit wolfish, and she laughed.

"So you think you can do that whenever now, huh?"

"I didn't even get to see you yesterday." The affairs at the community center were in a frenzy, with last-minute details, booths, and décor going up.

"At least everything's ready for the Festival of Trees on Friday," she said.

"Yeah, but then I'll be on graveyard duty for three weeks," he said, wrapping his arms around her and bringing her close, close to his heart.

"Who takes care of Porter while you're on graveyards?"

"I have someone who sleeps at the house with him," he said. "Adam worked it out with me and another guy— Phil Dryden, who loves to work graveyards. I only do three weeks every other rotation, and I don't go in until nine. I'm off by seven, so it's a ten-hour shift instead of twelve." He touched the tip of his nose to hers. "So I can get Porter to bed, and be there when he wakes up."

"Mm," she said, her eyes closed already.

"So can I kiss you now?" he asked.

"Oh, you might as well," she whispered, tipping up to meet his mouth. Kissing Lauren was almost an out-of-body experience for Trent, and he felt time lengthen into slow strands as they moved in tandem.

Someone cleared their throat, and Lauren ducked her head, breaking the kiss and hiding halfway behind Trent.

"Dinner's ready," Adam said, a laugh in his voice. "I'll tell them you need a minute?" He grinned and pointed to Trent's face. "Might want to wipe off that lipstick." He went back inside and said, "Yeah, they went for a walk. It'll be just a sec," before the door closed.

Trent started laughing, but quieted quickly when Lauren didn't. "What?" he asked.

"It's embarrassing," she said.

"It is?" Trent peered at her. "You're the one who's

supposed to be wearing lipstick." He wiped at his mouth, glad when he'd teased a smile out of her. "And it doesn't matter. They all know we're together anyway."

"That's true." Lauren ran her fingers through her hair and stood up straight. "I look okay?"

"Better than okay, sweetheart." He smiled at her, everything inside him softening.

"You know," she said slowly, taking a small step toward the door. "I could stay with Porter while you're on the graveyard shift."

Trent paused, not quite sure what to say. "Yeah?"

"Yeah, I mean, it's just sleeping, and he knows me."

He knew Randi too, but Trent didn't say that. Lauren opened the door and said, "Just something to think about," before she went inside.

Trent followed her and joined the group. Mabel pointed to the table. "Porter has made place cards for each of you. So find your spot, and let's get eating." She glanced at Trent and added in a voice that no one could hear over the movement of feet and the scuffing of chairs being pulled out, "And you still have lipstick on."

16

Lauren had never felt as much gratitude in her life as she did at that Thanksgiving dinner. She didn't know everyone at the table extremely well, but they were kind. They laughed quickly. Janey and Gretchen included her in their conversations and lunch plans, which she'd have to break later anyway.

She sat between Adam and Aunt Mabel, with Trent a few places away, right next to Porter. She could easily meet his eye across the table, and every time she did, a zing of attraction zipped up her spine.

The man had completely captivated her, and she felt like she'd jumped out of an airplane without a parachute.

"All right," Aunt Mabel said in her weathered voice once everyone had almost finished eating. "I'd like to have a few minutes where we talk about things we're grateful for." She beamed around at the people at the table. "I know you all from different things, times, and places, but you're all very dear to me." She patted Lauren's hand and then held it tight. "After I die, I want you all to get together and talk about how wonderful I am."

Everyone laughed, and Lauren did too, though a hitch of sadness hit her heart. She couldn't imagine Hawthorne Harbor without Aunt Mabel.

"After all," she continued. "Not a single one of you would be where you are without me."

They all consented with nods, and Adam leaned down and kissed Janey's temple. "She's right, you know. She told me not to let Janey push me away, and I listened."

"For once," Aunt Mabel said in a dry tone.

Lauren felt like an outsider to this conversation, to the love and happiness the other couples at the table were obviously involved in.

"She introduced me to Donna," Joel said, and Lauren smiled at the fondness in his voice, both for his wife and for Mabel. And Lauren knew that the shoes she had to fill at the Mansion were so much bigger than just running amazing events.

"So," Mabel said. "I'll start. I am grateful all of you chose to spend this holiday with me." She looked at Lauren. "You're next."

Lauren looked around the table, these faces ones she'd like to spend more time with, really get to know. "I'm grateful to be in Hawthorne Harbor."

As they continued around the table, a calm, peaceful feeling came over Lauren, especially when Trent said, "I'm grateful for a new deck and all the possibilities it brings to my back yard." He grinned at her, and Lauren's whole body flushed.

"That's it?" Adam asked. "Your deck?"

"It's going to complete the back yard," Trent said easily. "Right, bud?" He glanced at Porter next to him. "It's your turn. You gotta say something you're happy you have."

Porter took in a big breath and held it for a moment, the wheels in his head obviously turning. "The deck is awesome," he said. "But I'm happy Lauren lets me help her build it."

Gretchen and Janey zeroed in on her, but Lauren ignored the heavy weight of their gazes as she smiled at Porter. The activity finished, and Mabel said, "I'll put on the coffee."

The following morning, Lauren woke up in the dark, knowing she wouldn't be home until well after dark too. She lay in bed for a few moments, reliving yesterday's wonderful Thanksgiving dinner, the walk around the Mansion grounds as the sun went down, Trent's hand in hers, and how deeply he kissed her before driving off with his son.

No doubt about it, Lauren was falling fast for him. A moment of fear rumbled through her, but it fled quickly. No, her parents wouldn't approve, but Lauren knew Trent wasn't anything like Rick. And as soon as they met him, they'd know too.

She rolled over on her side and picked up her phone from the bedside table. Her mother still hadn't confirmed that they'd come for Christmas, and Lauren should probably tell Aunt Mabel if any of them were coming.

One family text, and one message to her mother, later, and Lauren got herself out of bed and into the shower. She had to be at the community center in an hour, and she'd be flitting from display to display until at least lunchtime, fixing last-minute and unexpected problems.

After she pulled her hair into a tight ponytail, she checked her phone. "Darrel, Eldon, and Byron are coming?" She read through the messages again, just to be sure.

We'll be there, Darrel's had said. I'm bringing Kimmy. Easy way to meet all the Magleby's at once, right?

Thanks for the invite! Eldon had texted. I'm coming with Byron. Right, B? Leaving on Christmas Eve about noon. Can we crash with you Lauren?

Leaving on Christmas Eve at noon, Bryon had said.

You can stay with me, Lauren sent. It'll be awesome to see you all!

Her mother had not answered, but she never had been

much of a morning person. Lauren stuffed her feet into her work boots and left the house so she'd have time to stop at Duality for coffee.

By the time she pulled into the community center, the early-morning walkers had arrived. The wind felt like needles against her face as she hurried toward the doors, and the warm rush that hit her when she went inside made her sigh.

Gene waited for her just inside the doors, and she said, "Hey, sorry I'm late."

"You're not late." They started walking toward the huge multi-purpose room where the Festival was set up. "Sabrina has been doing yoga at the crack of dawn, and I can't sleep once her alarm goes off." He yawned to punctuate the sentence and reached for the door handle ahead of Lauren.

She half-expected that they'd be the first two people in the showroom, but she should've known better. The room buzzed with activity, and Lauren almost turned and walked right back out.

"Okay," she said with a much less happy sigh. "Let's check in at the control room." She walked down the eight hundred aisle toward the back of the room, letting her gaze slide down the long row of gingerbread houses just before going through the door marked PERSONNEL ONLY.

She wasn't expecting to see Trent until later in the day,

but a keen sense of disappointment still hit her when she found Jason Zimmerman and Paul Hollister standing near one of the monitors.

They both glanced at her and Gene when they came in, both lifted their hands in a general greeting, and both turned back to the monitor as a unit. It was like they were programmed to act exactly the same, and she wondered if Trent had trained them for today.

"I think I'm supposed to have a radio," she said when she joined them.

"Oh, yeah," Jason said, turning away from the screen. He handed her one and one to Gene. "Frequency three. There are ten volunteers on the floor already. They all have radios too, and we'll all hear them when they call in. That way, if it's you they need, you'll know. And if it's us, we'll know." He gave her a smile and she returned it.

"Thanks." She'd sat down for two minutes before someone said, "I need electrical help on aisle six hundred, display six-seventy-two."

"You're up, Gene," she said with a smile. "Kam will be here about two."

Gene got up without complaint and left Lauren to sip her coffee in the much quieter control room. She thought about Trent, and if they might be able to have lunch together today. She'd take eating a hot dog with him while he walked the aisles if that was what it took to see him.

She got called out to the floor, and as the hour approached when the doors would open and the public would be let in, Lauren hoped for a few minutes of peace and quiet. She'd just reached the end of one of the aisles after fixing a simple structural problem when her phone buzzed.

She pulled it out of her pocket to see her mom had sent a text. *We'll be there, honey.* A little heart emoticon sat behind that, and Lauren felt her chest expand.

"They're coming." A sense of awe filled the words, and Lauren knew what it took for her mom to come back to Hawthorne Harbor, especially among all the Magleby's.

She sent off a quick text to Aunt Mabel so she'd know to expect six more Michaels family members, and then she typed out, *Thanks, Mom. I appreciate it. I want you to meet Trent and his son, Porter.*

Staring at her phone, waiting for her mother's response, enabled her to see Trent's text immediately when it came in.

Wilson's working the line. Come see!

Lauren glanced up, the thought of being in the same building as Trent intoxicating. Oh, yeah, she definitely had it bad for him, and as she strode down the aisle, past a dozen Christmas trees, she hoped she hadn't sacrificed the only part of herself she could never get back.

Her heart.

She went out the doors clearly marked EXIT and looked to her left. A long line of people stretched, standing as they waited for the doors to open.

She noticed movement, but it was on the other side of

the line. As she got closer, she could see Trent walking back and forth, down and around the line. On his way back, she saw Wilson, tongue out, eyes sharp, working.

The doors opened, and a general breath was released as the people started shuffling forward and into the event area. Lauren stood out of Trent's sight and watched him with his dog. The man clearly adored the canine, and a glow seemed to hover around him.

When half of the people had gone in, she walked over to him. "He's doing great."

When he saw her, his whole face brightened. "Look at him. I think he's ready to go to a real working unit."

Lauren smiled at him, his joy so obvious and so infectious. "You'll miss him, though, right?"

"Totally," Trent said, not even trying to deny it. "And another dog will have to step up and be the pack leader."

"Who'll do that?" she asked, walking with Trent as he moved with Wilson.

"Probably Brutus."

Her radio crackled, and someone needed help with a sign that had started to fall in one of the booths. When Gene said, "I'm doing a repair on aisle five hundred," Lauren rolled her eyes and lifted the radio to her mouth.

"I'm on my way," she said and let go of the button. "Can we try to grab lunch later?"

"Sure, yeah." Trent didn't look away from his dog.

"Great. See you then." Lauren walked away, desperate

to show she wasn't desperate for him to hold her close like he had the last few times they'd been together. After all, she'd already fallen so fast for him. Maybe a little distance would be a good thing, especially in public.

By lunchtime, her stomach was severely angry that she'd only given it coffee for breakfast, her back hurt from bending over to look under Christmas trees, and her patience for anyone who didn't have food in their hand was at an all-time low.

"I'm going to get something to eat," she said into her radio. "I'll be unavailable for an hour." She usually just grabbed something from one of the booths and ate it as she hurried from one thing to another, but today she was going to take a lunch—and not inside this building, where she'd been buried all day.

She took her pizza and soda outside, but the rain had started. Standing in the foyer between the outer doors and the inner doors, she ate her pepperoni and sausage pizza, watching the water sluice down the glass.

She could see her reflection in the watery glass, and she didn't look all that pleased. She wondered what it would be like to have her old secretary job back. For one thing, she wouldn't be working today, a tool belt around her waist and a piece of floppy pizza in her hand. She'd be shopping with friends and enjoying lunch at the bistro.

Then she'd go home and curl up in front of her fireplace and take a nap.

At least that was what she imagined her life would be like.

She turned away from her reflection, turning away from the thoughts too. She didn't want that old life, with that old job, and no confidence. In fact, when she'd had that life, she stood in front of windows and dreamed of this life she currently had.

"So be grateful for it," she muttered to herself. Good days came with the bad, she knew that. Her mother had always taught her that, and she'd had some good things happen today too—her family committing to come to the Mansion for Christmas, for one.

She didn't see Trent standing near the ropes anymore, and she wondered where he'd gone. He hadn't texted once all morning after she'd seen him working with Wilson, and he was probably too busy to sit down for a few minutes. She'd texted him twenty minutes ago, and he still hadn't responded.

With her pizza gone, and only ten minutes of her hour-long lunch with it, she wandered away from the Festival of Trees, just for a little quiet time. Everything in the showroom was loud, and she simply needed a break.

She found a couch around the corner and collapsed onto it. Her eyes drifted closed, and she thought she might be able to fall asleep right there. Before she could doze, she pulled out her phone and silenced it. She set a timer for forty-five minutes and made sure the radio was also muted. Then she lay down on the couch and got comfortable.

She wasn't sure how long she was asleep before she heard someone say her name. Her eyes jerked open to find Trent standing above her. "There you are," he said, a hint of anger in his voice. "I've been trying to get a hold of you."

Lauren scrambled to sit up, her heart pounding in her chest as her adrenaline spiked. She blinked, and Trent's normally passive, handsome face morphed into Rick's sharply angled face, his displeased eyes.

She blinked again, and everything changed back to Trent—except the eyes. "You shouldn't silence your phone like that," he said, sitting next to her on the couch.

"I wanted to sleep," she said, maybe a bit defensively. With Rick, she'd learned not to argue, because he simply mocked her. She hated hearing how he thought she sounded, so she'd learned to say nothing.

"I thought we were going to have lunch together."

"I texted you," she said, still trying to throw off the dregs of unconsciousness. She yawned and instinctively leaned away from him, like he was a cobra about to strike.

"I was busy."

"Well, I was busy now," she said, this time with a definite bite in her voice. Did he think she had to jump to his attention whenever he managed to get a text off?

Their eyes met, and Lauren felt a new kind of fire burning through her. Anger.

She hadn't felt angry in so long, and she almost wanted to feed the rage more fuel.

"I'm sorry I disturbed you," he said, his eyes just as sparking hot as hers. With that, he got up and walked away, leaving her on the couch to try to figure out what had just happened—and why she felt like taking a nap had turned into a crime.

17

Trent just needed to eat. And get out of this building. He felt confined to it, and he'd been looking forward to lunch with Lauren.

So maybe he was just disappointed. But as his feet put more and more distance between them, he knew he was angry with her. *Angry.*

And he hadn't felt angry with anyone in quite a while.

Sure, maybe God from time to time, but not another person he had to interact with on a daily basis. Not someone like Lauren, who he *wanted* to interact with whenever he could.

So what was wrong with him today?

He walked in the rain, his head bent and his police cap doing little to keep the rain off his face. Thoroughly soaked, he arrived at his cruiser and got in. The interior smelled like a wet dog, because he'd finished with Wilson about an hour ago and had taken the dog back to his house.

He hadn't had the stomach to make the four German shepherds stay in their outdoor kennel, so they were all currently cooped up in the kitchen, where they'd stay dry and warm. His mother had texted to say Porter was having a blast, and that they were making mac and cheese for lunch.

Trent's stomach roared, and he started the car and backed out of the parking space. He just needed to eat.

So he went through a drive-through and got a burger and fries. He ate it right there in the car, washing everything down with his favorite cola. And still he was annoyed that Lauren had silenced her phone and then fallen asleep.

She was the one who'd mentioned lunch. Didn't she know how difficult it was for him to organize his schedule to fit hers? He'd worked on the plans for the Festival of Trees for weeks, and he was late returning to the community center as it was.

He sighed and rested his forehead against the cold glass in his car. He wanted to take a nap too, but he couldn't. He had work to do.

So he drove back to the Festival and went in to relieve Lou so the man could have a lunch too. Jason and Paul had been replaced with two others, one of which was the Chief himself.

"Hey, Adam," he said as he approached the man standing guard at the entrance.

"There you are. Good lunch?"

"I guess." Trent didn't want to talk to anyone. "I'm on the floor next. I'll send Lou out."

Adam cocked his head as if he could see Trent's troubled thoughts. "Sounds good. I sent Gil to find you. He's probably in the control room."

"Great." Before Trent could walk away, Adam's hand shot out and touched his arm.

"You okay?"

Trent met his boss's eye, wanting to ask a million questions about women. He felt like he should know more than he currently did. He'd been married before, for crying out loud. But it had been a long time since those days, and he'd been busy trying to figure out how to live without Savannah and raise Porter by himself.

"Yeah," he simply said and walked away.

He found Lou in aisle three hundred, and said, "Time for your lunch, Lou. I'll take the floor."

"Thanks." Lou wore a look of utter gratitude, and he headed for the food booths. Trent wandered, seemingly looking at the trees, but he was really just watching for people or things that might become problems.

He saw Lauren working on something at one of the tree stations, but he turned around and went back the way he'd already come.

Why, he didn't know. Only that he didn't want to see her right then. A bit of shame sifted through him that he'd simply walked away from her. They'd been getting along so well for weeks, despite Trent's hang-ups about his first wife.

He finished his shift and went to Bell Hill to get Porter. Once on his mother's couch, he didn't want to get up again, so he asked, "Can I just stay here tonight? I have to be over to the community center again at one tomorrow, so I can cook breakfast in the morning."

His mom met his eyes with concern in hers. "You work too hard."

"Maybe," Trent said. But he had no other choice. He'd like airport security better than the small-town police force, but there wasn't an airport in Hawthorne Harbor. "But the dogs are doing well."

He remembered he couldn't stay. "I left the dogs in the kitchen," he said. "I have to go feed them and let them out." He sighed as he pushed himself to the edge of the couch. "Come on, Porty. We have to go."

"Let him stay," his mother said. "You're bringing him back tomorrow anyway, and this will save you the drive."

Trent looked back and forth between his mother and father. "You sure?"

"He's no trouble," his dad said. "Sleep in tomorrow. Your mom's right. You look tired."

Maybe that was why he'd snapped when Lauren hadn't responded to his texts and calls. Or maybe he'd been freaked out, because after Savannah's accident she hadn't been able to answer his phone.

Lauren's fine, he told himself as he stood and hugged his mom and then his dad. "All right, but tomorrow, you guys come over to the Festival, and we'll have dinner together. Okay?"

They agreed, and he went home to find that one of the shepherds had figured out how to open cupboards and drawers. Every one they could reach was open and several plastic containers had been chewed, as had an entire box of cold cereal.

"Really, guys?" he asked as he stood there and surveyed the damage. "And just when I thought you were ready to be shipped off to a unit, Wilson."

The pack leader whined, his nose pressed right up against the gate Trent used to keep them off his carpet.

"Let's go out," he said. "Then it's time for bed." He let the dogs into the back yard to take care of their business, filled their water and food bowls, and showered. His mind never strayed far from Lauren, and a pinch of guilt hit him in the chest.

As he lay down, all four dogs on the bed with him, he hoped sleep would claim him quickly. But it took its sweet time, forcing him to wonder if he'd gone a bit too fast with the beautiful general contractor. Maybe he wasn't quite ready to have someone too permanent in his life.

Or maybe, just maybe, he was afraid of losing

someone again. And if he didn't have someone, then they wouldn't get taken from him.

THE NEXT MORNING, TRENT DID SLEEP LATER THAN USUAL. Wilson woke him with a single bark, and Trent rolled out of bed to see the rain had stopped, at least for the time being. So he dressed in his running pants and a T-shirt, leashed the dogs, and took them down to the beach. In this weather, no one would mind if he took the shepherds off the leash.

He stretched while they ran around nearby, and then he called them all into line with him. With two dogs on each side, he started down the sand, hoping to run fast enough to leave his circular thoughts about Lauren behind.

That didn't work, and when he showed up later at the community center, it was like his gaze was drawn right to her construction truck parked in the circular drive.

So he just needed to talk to her.

He pulled out his phone and sent her a message. Would love to see you today. Are you at the Festival?

Of course she was; he was standing right beside her truck.

Yep.

Can you come outside for a few minutes or are you too busy?

Lauren took several minutes to respond, but when she did, she said, *Coming now.*

He barely had time to spin toward the doors before she came through them, her dark hair piled high on top of her head. She wore an unfriendly look as she approached, and she stopped about ten feet away and folded her arms. "Hello."

So he'd messed up. He knew enough about women to know that. "It's cold out here. Want to sit in your truck?"

"No," she said. "They have hot chocolate and coffee in the control room. Why don't you just come in there?"

He glanced over her shoulder. "Because there are other people in there."

She narrowed her eyes and took a step forward that felt menacing. "I don't appreciate being told I need to check my phone," she said. "Nor the fact that you acted like I was in the wrong by lying down during my lunch to rest."

Trent nodded. "I'm sorry. I may have over-reacted."

She paused, clearly not expecting him to apologize. "What?"

"You're right. I shouldn't have woken you. I was...." He swallowed, wishing his throat wasn't quite so sticky. "I panicked, okay? When my wife died, I called and texted her a bunch of times." His eyes met hers, and that anger burned through him again. "So when I couldn't get in touch with you, I may have freaked out a little. And then when I found you, I was...."

"Rude," she said, her voice soft and no longer accusatory.

"Yeah. That."

She sighed and reached into her pocket, extracting her keys a moment later. She unlocked the truck and started around to the driver's side. She got in, and Trent did too. With the heater blowing, he didn't think he'd lose his fingers to frostbite, but the chill between him and Lauren was still quite wintery.

"I may have over-reacted too," she finally said. "Remember Rick? Well, you acted just like he used to yesterday. And I didn't like it."

"I'm sorry," Trent said again.

"I mean, I know you're *not* him. He would never apologize, for one." She adjusted the heater vent so it was blowing on her better. "But it was still—I got angry. I'm not going back to the person who's panicked every time I miss a text. I won't do that. I'm busy too, and my busy is no less important than yours."

Trent hung his head and studied his hands. "Of course it's not." He really had no idea what she'd been through, and he didn't want to ever act like her ex again. "So maybe it was just a bad moment for both of us."

"I also didn't appreciate you walking away," she said. "That's not how things work in a relationship, Trent." She touched his arm, and he felt like she'd branded him.

He looked at her, hoping how badly he felt showed in his face. "I know. I—I made a mistake, and maybe we can just erase yesterday from our memories and try again today."

She softened and nodded before removing her hand and looking out the windshield.

"My parents are bringing Porter for dinner. Maybe, if the time is right, you can join us."

"Let's try for that," she said.

The tension between them broke, and Trent sighed. The strength of his feelings surprised him. He didn't want to walk away from Lauren, and he'd been genuinely upset when he couldn't get a hold of her, as if she'd been in an accident the way Savannah had.

It was all very confusing, and he hoped he'd be able to figure things out as they continued to get to know one another.

"I want to confess something," he said.

"Oh, yeah?"

"I don't particularly like being a cop." He met her gaze, and she looked surprised. "I worked airport security before coming back here, and I liked that better. And most of all, I want to train police dogs."

"Then do that," Lauren said, like making such a big career move could be so simple.

He thought of Adam, and how he couldn't just leave the Chief high and dry, especially during the Festival of Trees. He shook his head. "Just a confession. Nothing to be done about it." He reached for the door handle. "Let's go get some of that hot chocolate."

She tucked her hand into his as they walked toward the community center. "Trent, you really should do what you love. If it's not this, then do something else."

"I'll think about it," he said, because he certainly didn't want to keep talking about it. Not right now. He wasn't even sure why he'd told Lauren, other than he wanted to share parts of himself with her that he hadn't with anyone else.

A WEEK PASSED, AND THEN TWO, AND THE FESTIVAL OF Trees only had one more weekend before it would be taken down. And thankfully, Trent didn't have to work it, as he was on the graveyard shift starting Monday. He'd stay on the overnight shift until Christmas Eve, which was perfect timing, really.

His relationship with Lauren seemed to be back on track, but he found himself watching her more during the quiet moments they spent together. Rain and wind prevented her from finishing his deck completely, but she said it was about eighty percent done, and the railing and final staining just needed to be finished.

He wasn't concerned about it; after all, he knew where to find her to get the job done. Not only that, but he'd only paid for two-thirds of the deck, and she wouldn't get the rest without finishing to his satisfaction.

And tonight, she was coming to stay with Porter. His

regular nanny had seemed relieved when he'd called and said he was going to have Lauren stay overnight with Porter, so Trent felt good about the situation.

If only his heart would stop misfiring every third beat. He wasn't sure why that was happening, only that it somehow felt very up-close and personal to have Lauren sleep in his house.

The doorbell rang, and he nearly jumped out of his skin. Then he really did leap to his feet and hurry around the couch and down the hall to open the door for her. "You could've just come in," he said as he swung the door open. Then he saw her arms full of grocery bags, and he made to take some from her. "Let me help."

She smiled at him, that gentle smile that kept him awake at night thinking about her, and moved past him and into the house.

"What is all this?" he asked.

"Oh, I don't stay anywhere without proper reinforcements," she said. In his kitchen, she unpacked the soda, popcorn, and red licorice before turning to him. "Is there a cupboard I can put this in?"

Trent simply stared at her for a moment past comfortable. "Uh, yes," he said, jerking forward again. He felt like a robot whose batteries were dying, making herky jerky movements, some too close together and some too delayed. He opened the first cupboard he came to, but it was full of plates. "Uh...."

Lauren laughed and started opening drawers in the

island. "What about in here?" she asked, peering down into the bread drawer. "It's almost empty, and it's just a couple of boxes of popcorn."

"Sure," he said. "You can obviously put the soda in the fridge." The collar on his police uniform scratched, and he itched his neck. "So Porter's already had a bath. His homework is done. I usually put him to bed before I go, but he said he wanted to see you."

"That's fine." She stepped up to him and ran her hands up his arms, clasping her hands behind his neck. "Have you forgotten that I've put him to bed many times? Remember how you fall asleep on the couch a lot?" She smiled at him, and some of Trent's nervous energy fled.

"I don't know why I'm so keyed up," he said.

She lifted up onto her toes and kissed him, and Trent took her comfort, her calmness, her safety and security as he kissed her back. The kiss was sweet, and she pulled away after only a few seconds. "Okay?" she whispered.

He nodded, noting how well she fit in his arms. "Let me get Porter." He walked down the hall to the boy's room, where he played with a set of cars on the floor, two dogs keeping him company.

"Porty, Lauren's here." He stood halfway in the room and halfway out. "You can only stay up for a little bit."

Porter jumped to his feet and went racing past Trent, a toy car in each hand. Trent stayed in the room with the dogs, listening to his son practically yell as he said, "Heya, Lauren. Look at my cars."

Her response wasn't as clear, because her voice was softer. Trent took a deep breath. "I'm not crazy, right?" he asked Brutus and Tornado.

Tornado cocked his head, but Brutus got up and trotted down the hall after Porter. So Trent went back into the kitchen too, only to find Lauren moving around his house as if she'd lived there for years, chatting with Porter about the Christmas crafts they were making for their Christmas Around the World celebration.

"And we're doing gingerbread houses next Friday," he said. "Right before the break. You should come."

"That does sound fun," Lauren said, not making a commitment at all.

"I have to go to work," Trent said, and he hugged Porter before setting him up on the barstool. "Not too late. Promise me."

"Not too late," Porter repeated.

Lauren followed him down the hall to the front door, kissing him quickly and said, "I promise not to let him stay up too late either."

Trent managed to force a smile to his face, and then he stepped outside to go to work. He went around back to get the dogs, who needed practice working in the dark, and slid open the door to let the two inside out. He got all four of them in the back of his truck without a problem. He sat in the cab and watched his house for a minute. Lauren was more than capable with Porter, and he was so glad she'd offered to stay with him.

"And she said she didn't like kids," Trent said quietly, deciding to stop stalking his own house and get over to the station. He couldn't help thinking that this could be his future if he and Lauren stayed serious and eventually got married.

She'd be here in the mornings, the afternoons, the evenings, and overnight. And he could kiss her good-bye and good morning when he returned. As he pulled into the lot behind the station, he realized he'd just had a tiny glimpse of what his life could be like with Lauren Michaels in it permanently.

And he really liked it.

He really liked *her*.

"Takes more than like to make a marriage," he said to Brutus as he got out of the truck and approached the tailgate. He paused as he sorted through the leashes, thinking that he could see himself falling in love with Lauren.

A bit of fear tripped through him, and he called the dogs to come down from the back of the truck. He'd wanted a new woman in his life, wanted a mother for Porter. He supposed he hadn't thought through everything as thoroughly as he should have, because he'd never considered that he'd fall in love with anyone but Savannah.

His sister's words from weeks ago plagued him as he walked the dogs into the station and over to his desk. *She's not who I pictured you with.*

Trent decided he didn't care. He liked spending his

time with Lauren, and it didn't matter what anyone else thought.

He hated the graveyard shift, because while there was crime in Hawthorne Harbor, it definitely slowed down between two and five a.m. The boredom was enough to kill even the most diligent cop, and Trent spent his time with the dogs in the yard. That, at least, passed the time much faster than anything else he'd tried.

By the time he returned home, he was ready for bed. But it was only six-thirty, and one step inside the house told him that both Lauren and Porter were still asleep. So he fed the dogs on the partially finished back deck and kept them outside while he set coffee to brew.

As the day started to lighten, he heard movement coming from down the hallway. A few minutes later, Lauren appeared, looking soft and fresh from sleep. The sight made him deliriously happy, and Trent pulled two mugs from the cupboard with a "Good morning."

"Hey." She sat at the bar and rubbed her eyes.

"You were up too late, weren't you?" He watched her with one eye while he got out the cream and sugar.

"No," she said, but a yawn immediately followed it. "Maybe until ten or so."

"He's going to be a bear."

"He promised he wouldn't be."

"Right." Trent leaned his weight against the counter opposite of her. "Just like you both promised he wouldn't stay up too late." He wasn't sure if he should smile or stay stern. Porter would be a complete bear by lunchtime, and his teacher would have to deal with it.

"It wasn't that late," she insisted, nodding toward the coffee pot. "Are you going to pour me some of that or what?"

Trent busied himself with pouring her coffee, and he watched as she added both cream and sugar to the black liquid. He wanted to have something to share with her, but his mind was blank.

"What'd you do last night?" she asked.

"Nothing," he said. "The graveyard shift is the worst."

"How did Wilson do with the ball in the dark?"

"Great. Brought it back every time." Trent needed to get his portfolio together and get it out to some agencies, because Wilson was ready to work on a real canine team. He poured himself a cup of coffee, which was probably a mistake. If he drank this, he wouldn't get to sleep until at least noon, and then he'd only get three hours of sleep before he had to pick up Porter.

So he set his mug on the counter and said, "I'm going to go check on Porty. He should be getting up soon."

Lauren nodded, and he felt her eyes on him as he walked away. His son snored in his bed, and Trent watched him for a minute. A book sat on his nightstand. Trent picked it up and didn't recognize it. In fact, he never read to his son. He hadn't even thought of it.

But Lauren had obviously brought this book—*Captain Underpants*—for Porter, and he found one of the pages had been dog-eared. Trent wasn't sure why the book bothered him. It was a book, and it was a sign that Lauren had thought about his son and tried to bring something she thought he would like.

So why did Trent feel like he wasn't doing a good job as Porter's father?

He set the book down and rubbed his son's back. "Porter," he said in almost a whisper. "It's time to get up, bud."

Porter groaned and rolled toward Trent, blinking the sleepiness out of his eyes. "Hey, Daddy."

Trent sat on the edge of his son's bed. "Hey, bud. Did you have fun last night?"

Porter sat up and gave Trent a hug. Trent held the small child in his arms, feeling lucky and inadequate at the same time. "I love you, bud," he said, his voice rough around the edges. He wasn't all that great at expressing his emotions, even to his son. It was a miracle he'd gotten married the first time.

"Lauren made popcorn," Porter said as he released Trent. "And then she melted butter and poured it all over it, and put on this cinnamon and sugar stuff, and she said it was called churro popcorn."

"Sounds delicious," Trent said. "She said you stayed up until ten."

"I won't be cranky," Porter said, his eyes turning into those puppy dog eyes that begged for food.

"If Miss Terry emails or calls, you'll be in so much

trouble." Trent gave his son a stern look. "Lauren won't be able to stay with you anymore."

"I like her," Porter said. "I'll be good, I promise."

Trent wanted to point out that he'd already broken one promise, but he was tired and just wanted to go to bed. "All right. Well, let's get up and get ready. I'll go fry you an egg."

18

Lauren didn't want to leave Trent's house, and she wasn't entirely sure why. But it felt wonderful and comfortable to be sitting in his kitchen, sipping coffee he'd made and poured for her.

He returned from waking Porter and said, "Did you want breakfast? I'm making eggs for Porter."

She declined and slipped off her barstool. "I better head home and get ready for the day."

"Yeah? What are you working on now?" He unhooked a pan from the rack hanging above the island.

"I just signed a new basement," she said. "It's huge too, from one of those massive houses out on the bluff."

"That's great."

"Yeah, indoor job," she said. "Though I am a bit worried about it running into our Christmas plans."

Trent pulled open the fridge. "Go over those again with me?"

Lauren had told him at least three times, but she'd go over it a dozen more if it meant he'd be there. Him and Porter. So she moved into his personal space as he turned with a carton of eggs in his hands.

She wrapped her arms around him, thrilled when he received her into his embrace. "My whole family is coming," she said. "I've told them all about you."

Trent looked so, so tired, but she thought she also caught a flicker of panic in his expression. "It's a Christmas dinner, right?"

"Right. My brothers are coming on Christmas Eve. My parents are coming on the twenty-third. So you can meet them in stages."

He leaned down and kissed her, and while Trent had never spoken about his feelings for her, Lauren could definitely feel them in the way his mouth moved against hers. Lauren let herself get caught up in him, the taste of him, the smell of him, the very nearness of him. And she felt herself falling, and all she could do was hope he would be there to catch her.

She broke their connection and looked at him. "You're still okay to do all of that?"

"Mm hm." He pressed his cheek to hers, and they just breathed together. Lauren wanted to tell him how she was feeling, but so many emotions ran through her she didn't trust herself to speak.

"Dad, I can't find my shoes."

Trent stepped away from Lauren and said something, but she didn't catch what. She hoped her late night with Porter wouldn't get him in trouble, because then Trent wouldn't trust her with his son again.

"I saw them in the closet," she called after them, her mind finally starting to work again. Sure enough, Trent found the shoes there, and Lauren gave Porter a hug. "I have to go. I'll see you tonight, okay?"

Porter leaned his forehead against Lauren's and whispered, "Daddy says we can't stay up late or you can't stay with me."

"Then we'll make sure you're in bed by nine tonight, okay?"

He nodded, and she straightened. Trent was busy with the pan on the stove, but she knew he'd seen her exchange with his son. She lifted her hand in a wave and said, "See you guys tonight."

"'Bye," they said together, one low voice and one high, and Lauren's heart sang with joy.

Outside, she stood on the top step and vowed to herself that she'd follow Trent's rules for his son. After all, she wasn't the boy's mother, and if the situation had been reversed, she'd be bugged if her babysitter just did whatever she wanted.

And she loved both of the males inside this house. A smile touched her lips, and though the winter temperatures had her breath wisping out of her mouth in white clouds, she felt warm from head to toe.

Because she was in love with Trent Baker.

LAUREN WORKED ALONE IN THE BASEMENT OF THE HOUSE ON the bluff, measuring and marking, cutting and constructing. It had taken a couple of days just to get everything hauled into the area, but now that she was set up, the work was moving quickly. If her pace held, she'd have the basement framed and insulated by the end of the week.

She'd done enough basements to know when she needed to focus and when she could let her mind wander. So she concentrated when at the saw and with the measuring tape in her hand, but she thought about Porter and Trent while she hammered the studs into place.

Porter especially lingered in her mind. Why had she thought she didn't like kids? *Maybe you haven't met the right ones*, Trent had said.

But Lauren knew that everything stemmed back to Rick. *He* hadn't liked children, and she'd known from their third date that he didn't want kids. So maybe she'd just told herself for so long that she didn't want them either.

By the time she returned to Trent's that afternoon, she was tired of measuring, cutting, and nailing. But she put up a section of the railing before he and Porter arrived home from school.

"Heya," Porter said, immediately picking up his child-sized hammer. "I didn't get in trouble at school at all today."

She beamed at him, more relief than she thought she'd feel pouring through her. She glanced at Trent, who wore his police officer stern expression. "That's great, bud. We'll be sure to get to bed on time tonight."

"So can I help?" A gust of wind almost blew the boy's words away.

Lauren nodded. "I'm just about to cut the next section."

"It can wait," Trent said, finally moving forward and putting his arm around her. "You look tired."

"So maybe I need to get to bed earlier tonight too." She relaxed into his side, definitely more exhausted than she thought.

"Porter's going to lay down for an hour."

"Dad—"

"We already talked about it, bud." Trent cut him a glare. "You can too, if you'd like. I'll make dinner."

Lauren gazed out across his yard, most of the greenery brown now. It was still beautiful, and though the wind whipped and another storm would be here within the hour, Lauren felt more comfortable than she ever had.

She went with Porter and Trent inside, and the two boys disappeared down the hall. She heard them arguing, but she kept herself busy with getting water and cleaning up from her long day of work. Maybe Trent would put off making dinner and just hold her on the couch until she dozed off.

By the time Trent returned, he looked tired too. He didn't say anything, and the tension in the air nearly suffocated Lauren.

"If he's not tired, he doesn't have to take a nap," she said.

Trent whipped his gaze to her, and it utterly scathed her. "He *is* tired. That's why he's acting like that."

"Okay, I'm just saying—"

"Well, don't. He's not your son, and I think I know him a lot better than you do."

His words lashed her insides, and any thought of curling into the couch with him and kissing away the afternoon vanished. She nodded, tight little movements of her head. Tears pricked her eyes, and the thought of staying here made her chest tighten until she couldn't breathe.

"I'm going to run home and shower," she managed to say.

"Lauren," he said, not an ounce of regret in his voice.

"No, it's fine." She waved him back. "I just feel itchy from the insulation." What a liar she was. She hadn't even touched the insulation yet, and Trent seemed to know it. Still, he let her go, and Lauren wept as she drove from his house to hers.

So maybe she shouldn't be telling him how to raise his son. *Bad move*, she told herself, finally getting enough control of her emotions to make the tears stop. She sniffed and wiped her eyes, pulling into her driveway in control of herself.

Inside, she went straight into the bedroom and laid down. Maybe she was acting the way she was because she was tired too. After all, she hadn't cried over anything in years—since leaving Rick.

Then, it seemed like she'd never stop crying. But she had. She started working with a therapist and examining what she really believed, what was true and what wasn't, and she'd come out a different version of the Lauren she'd been.

She didn't want Trent to be upset with her, so before she allowed herself to truly calm enough to doze, she sent him a quick text. *I'm sorry.*

Hours later, she still hadn't heard from him, and it was almost time for her to get over to his house so he could go to work. She assumed that was still the plan, so she slathered peanut butter on a couple pieces of bread and grabbed an apple from the fridge.

She finished eating just as she arrived at his house, only to find his truck already gone. Confusion and doubt raced through her. Had he taken Porter to his sisters? His mothers? Maybe they were just out with the dogs, but the rain splashing the windshield suggested otherwise.

She parked in his spot and dashed up to the front

door. The doorbell sounded too loud amidst the rain, and it took several long moments for Betsy to answer the door. Lauren stood there and stared, unsure of what to make of this new development.

"He got called in suddenly," she said, gesturing for her to come in. She did, stepping onto his floor and starting to drip everywhere. "He said you'd be by soon, and I said it was no problem."

"Oh," Lauren finally managed to say. She searched her brain for her husband's name and couldn't find it. "How's your husband?"

She offered a kind smile, but it was the kind that said she was tired of answering the same questions all the time. "He's doing better tonight, which is why I could come."

"I would've come," Lauren said. Why hadn't Trent just called her? She lived ten minutes away, and watching Betsy put on her shoes and then her coat, it had honestly probably taken the older woman at least that long to make it over here from next door.

"I was here with dinner when the call came in," she said. "So it was no problem to stay." She gave Lauren a warm smile and paused in her preparations to leave. "So, how are you and Trent getting along?"

Lauren put a plastic grin on her face. "Just great." She nodded like her statement needed extra emphasis. "Yep. Real nice."

Which was mostly true. They'd been getting along so well, with a few minor bumps that all couples had. Right?

All she knew was that she thought so, and she didn't necessarily want to talk about it with his next-door neighbor, a woman she'd met once and didn't know.

"Well, hang in there, dear." She stood and patted Lauren's hand. "Porter's in bed already, and Trent said he'd call you later."

"All right." Lauren said, the papery quality of Betsy's skin so like Aunt Mabel's.

"Trent can be prickly sometimes," she said. "Don't take it too seriously. I've been telling him for years to lighten up." With that, Betsy made her way to the front door, where she pulled up the hood on her coat and stepped into the storm.

Lauren followed her and stood on the porch to make sure she got home okay. Once she was safely inside her own house, Lauren returned to the warmth of Trent's home. She loved this place where she'd spent so much time with him and his son.

She ran her fingers along the back of the couch where they'd cuddled together after dinner, where he'd fall asleep and she'd hold his hand and dream of that being their reality all the time.

Maybe he didn't want that. "Maybe he just needs more time to get used to the idea."

As soon as the words left her mouth, she sucked in a breath. How many times had she said that while waiting for Rick to do something she wanted? First, it was to put a diamond ring on her finger. Then it was to set a date—which had never actually happened.

She'd always told her mom that maybe he needed more time to think through the idea, make sure he liked it.

She pulled out her phone and sent him another text. *Made it to your house. Betsy went home. Porter's asleep.* Her fingers hovered over the screen. She wanted to tell him she would've come had he called, but she didn't want to add to his stress or make him feel like he'd done something wrong.

She shook the old Lauren's thoughts away. She got to have feelings too, and they were valid.

I would've come whenever you wanted. Why didn't you call me?

She sent the message without second-guessing herself and then dialed her mom. With Christmas just shy of two weeks away, Lauren should probably check with Aunt Mabel on the state of the Mansion and the dinner.

Knowing Mabel, the Mansion would be decked out from floor to ceiling with wreaths and trees and garland. But Lauren should still check with her. *Tomorrow*, she told herself as her mom's line started to ring.

"Hey, baby," her mother said. "How are you?"

Every emotion Lauren had been feeling that day rushed at her, choking her words from coming out.

"Lauren?" Her mother's concern could be heard from miles away.

"Hey, Mom," she said through a tight throat. Her mother would be able to hear the emotion in it.

"What's wrong? Did something happen with Trent?"

So many things had happened with Trent, and Lauren didn't even know where to start. "I don't know, Mom. I like him so much." Another lie, but this one was necessary. Wasn't it? She knew her mother worried about her, and she didn't want to admit she'd fallen in love with a man who might not be ready for another wife.

All at once, Lauren realized what she'd been fearing and doubting. That she was more than ready to move to the next stage of her life with him, but that for Trent, he might still be struggling with the concept of letting go of Savannah and taking hold of Lauren.

"Well, what's going on?" her mom asked, kindness in her voice where there had been disapproval of a relationship with Trent before.

Lauren told her, ready to be reprimanded. She could handle the truth, and she could change. Heaven knew she'd done plenty of that over the last six years.

"You two should probably have a conversation about parenting," her mom suggested. "If he's not interested in you disciplining Porter, you should know. He *is* the boy's father, and well, those *are* his decisions to make. You need to honor them."

"I know," Lauren said, but really, she only knew intellectually. She didn't have children of her own, or a past spouse, or any of the things Trent was dealing with. She took a deep breath, feeling more settled now. "Thanks, Mom."

"We'll see you soon, okay?"

Lauren nodded and sniffed. "Okay. Love you, Mom."

"I love you, Lauren."

The call ended, and Lauren let her arm drop to the couch. She sat cross-legged in front of the TV she hadn't switched on. She had taken a nap that afternoon and didn't feel physically tired. Just mentally and emotionally exhausted.

So when Trent's text of, *Betsy was already there* came in, she read it and swiped it away. Her phone buzzed again, probably him with another message. But she didn't read it. She curled into herself on the couch and closed her eyes, imagining the way Trent would come home from the graveyard shift and kiss her awake once they were married and living in the same house together.

She must've dozed off right there on the couch, because the next thing she knew, she woke up to the sound of Porter screaming.

19

Trent stared at his phone, willing Lauren to answer him. The dead time had arrived and it was only nine-thirty. The night stretched ahead of him, and he was in no mood for it. He thought about walking across the street to the firehouse, where surely there'd be good food and probably a dance party happening.

Why they didn't have barbecues and big-screen televisions in the police department, he didn't know.

What he did know was that he and Lauren needed to talk. He hadn't liked her keeping Porter up, and when she'd suggested his own son didn't need to take a nap, Trent's anger had returned in full force.

He'd been thinking about it since he'd woken that afternoon to go get his son from school. No, he hadn't gotten in trouble with Miss Terry. But Trent knew Porter, and the boy was tired. Did it really matter if a six-year-old didn't want to lie down for an hour?

No. No, it did not. Trent was the adult, and once Porter had gotten up, he'd been back to his playful self.

He looked at his phone again, his question burning into his retinas. Should I bring breakfast back to the house and we can talk before Porter wakes up?

Maybe she didn't want to talk. Maybe she'd go get Betsy and wouldn't even be there when Trent returned.

"Trent, where are those files on the Bighorn case?"

Trent startled away from his thoughts and his device. He looked up at Adam, who should've gone home hours ago. "Uh, right here." He moved a few folders on his messy desk and handed a stack to the Chief.

"Thanks." He turned away and then twisted back. "Thanks for coming in early."

"Yeah, of course."

"I'm going to take these home with me."

"Good idea." Trent flashed him a smile that didn't stay on his face for more than a second. He flipped his phone over and over, but it didn't chime or buzz. So she was going to ignore him. Surely she wasn't asleep yet, but Trent wasn't really sure. He hadn't answered her right away, and maybe she'd gone straight to bed after texting him.

Determined not to spend his ten-hour shift obsessed with hearing from Lauren, he set his phone face-down on his desk and started working on the report from the incident he'd been called to that evening.

He could barely read his own handwriting, but he managed to make it through his notes, transferring them into the file. Then he went through the witness statements and was about to start on the other statements from the man and woman involved in the domestic dispute when a flashing blue light caught his eye.

Hesitating, he watched it blip on and off a few more times before he picked up his phone. Not only had Lauren texted, but she'd called. Twice.

He opened her text first and his heart was the next thing that started blipping when he saw the words. *Porter's hurt. Going to the hospital. Please call me.*

His chair skidded across the floor when he stood so suddenly. "Adam," he said, his voice barely loud enough to leave his throat. But the Chief had gone home; his office sat in darkness.

Trent's partner for the night was Gil Henderson, and he was probably with the man they'd brought in for more questioning. Jason Zimmerman was his normal partner while Trent was on graveyards, and he'd been called in too.

The two of them could handle anything else that happened tonight, Trent was sure of it. In his haste to get over to the witness rooms, he left his jacket behind. He found both men in the room, and he hesitated again.

But this was his son.

He knocked on the door and said, "Guys, sorry to interrupt. I need to talk to you both for a quick second."

Jason and Gil looked at him with surprise, but Trent didn't care. He couldn't wait much longer, and the panic built up inside him until he felt sure he'd explode. They must've seen it, because they both came out quickly.

"What's going on? Your face is white," Jason said.

"Porter's at the hospital," he said, forcing the words past the lump in his throat. "I have to go."

"Of course," Gil said. "Go."

Trent didn't wait for anyone else to say anything. He just turned and strode away, hearing Jason as he said, "I'll call the Chief and let him know."

"And the dogs are outside," Trent said, turning back.

"We got 'em," Gil said. "Go."

Trent had to backtrack to his desk for his wallet and keys, and then he got behind the wheel of the cruiser and put the lights on. He had to get to the hospital as fast as possible.

Everything in his body was tight, tight, and the sob that wanted to come out of his mouth felt stuck halfway between his gut and his throat. This couldn't be happening. Could it? He'd already lost Savannah. He couldn't lose Porter too.

And what in the world had happened? He'd gotten a text from Betsy just after eight that said Porter was asleep already. All Lauren had to do was not wake him up and go to bed herself.

Trent parked in the pick up lanes and left the lights on as he dashed inside. There were some perks to living in a small town—the hospital wasn't that big either. A big arrow pointed to the emergency room, where all inquiries were to be handled this late at night.

He sprinted that way, the desperation and panic at an all-time high. *Calm down*, he told himself. *Calm. Calm.* He was extraordinarily gifted at keeping a calm head with the dogs, with difficult people, and with chaotic situations.

But when it was his own life, he wasn't rational at all.

He'd felt this frenzied in Seattle too, and he'd been hoping and praying he'd never have to go through it again. It didn't seem fair that he was here tonight when he'd already identified one body in his lifetime.

"Porter Baker," he said, panting, when he arrived at the emergency room check-in desk. "He was brought in? Is he here?"

"Just a moment, Trent," Alice said, clicking away on her computer. "He was brought in by Lauren Michaels. Thirty-five minutes ago."

"What's wrong? Where is he?" *Thirty-five minutes ago* rebounded from one ear to the other. Had he been working on his reports that long? Why had he set his phone face-down? He never did that.

"Curtain seven." She stood as if Trent had never been to the ER before. Maybe not this one, and maybe not for a while, but he could open a door and find the numbers by the curtains.

He didn't really have to search that hard. His son's crying floated down the hall toward him like a siren's call, and he ran that way.

Crying's good, his brain told him, but he was in such a panic that he barely heard it.

He pulled the curtain open and tried to take in the whole scene at once. Porter sat on the bed, Lauren holding him tight against her chest. The doctor and the nurse both stood in front of them, and there was too much blood on the doctor's hands to calm Trent.

Lauren glanced over her shoulder at him, her eyes wide. "Your daddy's here," she said, her voice calm and quiet.

That got everyone to look at him, and Trent took a deep breath to try to find his center. But it was way out of whack, especially when he saw the bandage on his son's forehead, and he just wanted to know what had happened.

"Hold still, Porter," the doctor said. "Officer, we're almost done here." He focused on the work in front of him. "Then Jules will get your boy cleaned up and you'll be able to talk to him."

"What happened?" he asked, his voice sounding like he'd swallowed frogs and only knew how to croak.

"Porter got up to go to the bathroom," Lauren said, her voice almost a monotone. "He dropped the glass on the floor, and it broke. He stepped on the glass. That's why Doctor Burl is putting stitches in his foot. And he fell when that happened, so he got a little banged up because of that." She held him very tight. "But he is the bravest boy in the world, and we're almost done." She hummed, which somehow calmed Trent too. "Almost done, baby. Almost done. You're doing great."

Porter continued to cry, but it wasn't as horrible as Trent had first heard it. Or maybe he'd been imagining it to be worse. He wasn't sure.

Relief flowed through him with the strength of river rapids, and he just wanted to be the one holding Porter close and telling him he was doing great.

"Jules," Dr. Burl said, finally leaning back. He had a pair of tweezers in his fingers, and he turned back to his tray of tools before Trent could get too good of a look at them. The nurse worked for a few seconds with the doctor removed his gloves and put them in the hazardous waste bin.

"You'll have to stay off that foot for a while, bud." He grinned down at Porter. "Think you can do that?"

Porter nodded, and Dr. Burl looked at Trent and then Lauren. "It's probably best if he doesn't wear shoes for a few days. After that, he might need a crutch for a week or so. The stitches heal fast."

"Will he have to get them out later?" Lauren asked, and Trent simply stared at her. He had no questions in his brain. He simply felt numb.

"They dissolve," Dr. Burl said. "So nope." He tousled Porter's hair. "And you'll have a headache, but I'll write a

prescription for that. Where do you want me to send it?"
He looked at Lauren, who looked at Trent.

"Uh...Bushman's," he said, finally getting his mind to
catch up to the conversation.

"They aren't open until morning, but we have a couple
things we can send home with him." Dr. Burl turned to
Jules and said something, and she nodded.

"All right," she said with a bright smile. "You're all
done." She looked at Lauren as she pulled off her gloves.
"You guys can stay as long as you like. But he can go home
whenever you're ready."

"Thank you," Lauren said, and the medical staff
turned to leave.

"Thank you," Trent blurted after them, almost afraid
to be left alone with Lauren and Porter. But once he was,
he moved in front of his son and crouched down. "Hey,
bud. Hey."

Porter started crying anew, and Trent took him from
Lauren, who ducked her head and slid off the bed. Trent
took her spot and held his son right against his heart.
Thankfully, Lauren followed the doctor and the nurse
before Trent started crying too.

"It's okay," he said to Porter. "Everything's fine." He let
the silence in the hospital flow over him, using it to find
some sense of reason and get his emotions under
control.

When they'd both finally quieted, he stood up and
said, "Let's go home."

He found Lauren in the waiting room, and she jumped to her feet when they came out. "I'll take him," Trent said.

"I can follow you," she said. "Do you need to go back to work?"

He hadn't checked his phone since leaving the station, but he couldn't imagine something had happened that Jason and Gil needed him for. Shaking his head, he headed for the main entrance. Lauren separated from him at some point, but he caught sight of her headlights behind him after only a couple of blocks.

"Does it hurt?" he asked.

"Yeah," Porter said.

"I didn't get that stuff from the doctor," Trent said.

"I bet Lauren did."

Trent frowned at the night in front of him, but his son was probably right. Lauren had likely gotten the painkillers, and he'd be able to get more at the pharmacy in the morning.

He pulled into his driveway and hurried around to the passenger side to get his son out. He took him up the steps and through the front door, which was still slightly ajar. Once he got him settled in bed, he went back out to the kitchen, where Lauren stood with a cup of water and a couple of pills. "Can he swallow those?"

"Yes," Trent said, not quite ready to look her in the face. He returned to his son's room and watched him swallow the medicine. He sat in the chair beside the bed and picked up the book he'd seen that morning.

"Does Lauren read to you?" he asked.

"Just last night," Porter said. "She wasn't here tonight." He closed his eyes, his face tear-streaked. And with that bandage on his son's head, Trent had never felt more like a failure in his whole life.

He was supposed to protect Porter. Be there when he needed him. And he hated that he hadn't been able to do anything for his son tonight.

He watched him until he fell asleep, and then he put the book back on the bedside table and left the room as quietly as possible.

He half-hoped Lauren would be gone, but she sat at the bar in the kitchen, looking at her phone. "How is he?" she asked when Trent entered.

"He's fine," he said, suddenly feeling like he was carrying the weight of the world.

"Are you going to stay?"

"I'll call in," he said. "So yeah."

"Okay." She got down off the barstool. "Then I'll go. See you later." She moved over to the recliner and picked up her jacket. He hadn't noticed her wearing it at the hospital.

She was halfway to the door when he said, "I'm going to call Randi," he said. "She'll come stay with him tomorrow night." Or he'd take the night off.

A long silence followed, and then Lauren's footsteps sounded as she returned to the kitchen. "I don't mind staying with him. I would've come earlier tonight if you'd called."

He nodded, a war waging inside him. He finally looked up and into her dark brown eyes. They were filled with confusion and hurt and exhaustion, much the way he felt. "I don't—"

"This was an *accident*, Trent. You get that, right?"

He shook his head, unable to make his thoughts line up. "Porter never had any accidents with Randi."

She made an angry scoffing sound and said, "You know, the proper thing to say here would be thank you. Thank you, Lauren, for getting my son to the hospital quickly. Thank you for driving him while he bled all over your car. Thank you for cleaning up the bathroom while I sat with him and watched him fall asleep."

The anger in her voice wasn't hard to hear. Trent didn't dare look at her, and he didn't speak either.

She moved in front of him, forcing him to meet her eye again. "You don't think I can be a good mother."

Trent shook his head. "That's not it."

"Then what?"

"You said you didn't like kids."

"And you said maybe I hadn't met the right ones." She stabbed her finger toward the hall. "I love that little boy, and no, I'm not his mother. And I don't know him as well as you do. But I did a good job taking care of him tonight."

"It's not your job to do." Trent wasn't sure why he was pushing Lauren away, only that everything in his life had been simpler before she'd entered it. And he craved that simplicity. Then, at least, he'd know what to expect.

"So...what are you saying?"

"Nothing," he said, looking away again.

"Will it ever be my job to take care of him?" Lauren asked, and Trent didn't know how to answer that question. When he said that, she emitted another angry sound and walked away.

Right down the hall and out the front door, the slam of it behind her sounding very final. In fact, it sent a crack right through his heart and made the tears that had come earlier reappear.

20

"So we'll put you and Trent and Porter over here." Aunt Mabel moved around the table and indicated three seats.

Lauren looked up from the clipboard where she'd been making notes. "Oh, uh, Trent and Porter aren't coming."

Aunt Mabel whipped her head to Lauren. "What do you mean?"

"I mean, I don't think he'll come." She squirmed under the weight of her great aunt's glare. So she hadn't told anyone about what had happened at Trent's four nights ago. It wasn't a federal crime.

"Did he say he wouldn't be coming?"

They weren't exactly talking. "Um, no, he didn't, but I haven't spoken to him in days, and I don't think he'll just show up to this."

Aunt Mabel's eyes softened and she came closer. "What happened?"

"He called the nanny and had her come watch Porter." Lauren's heart twisted, and those stupid tears that had been plaguing her at odd times chose now to inflict themselves upon her. "He doesn't think I'd be a good mother."

He hadn't said those exact words, but Lauren couldn't find another explanation for his dismissal of her after Porter's accident. And he never had said thank you. Not once. For almost anything.

"Nonsense," Aunt Mabel said. "You'll be a great mom to that little boy."

Lauren had started to think so too, but that dream had cracked the night Trent had said he didn't know if she'd ever be able to take care of Porter in a maternal capacity. How had she fallen in love with him when he obviously had stayed on solid ground?

"He doesn't think so," she said, turning away so Aunt Mabel wouldn't see her cry. The tears were there in her voice anyway. "He said he doesn't know if I'll ever get to be Porter's mom." She gave up then and twisted back to her great aunt.

"And I'm stupid, and I went and fell in love with both of them."

Aunt Mabel wrapped her arms around Lauren, and she was surprisingly strong for an elderly woman. "Come on, now. Surely you misunderstood."

Lauren didn't think so. *It's not your job to do.* There

wasn't much gray area there, was there? She was exhausted, not having slept well since leaving Trent's house days ago, and she couldn't keep thinking about this. It hurt too much, and she couldn't keep breaking down.

She clung to her great aunt for a few more seconds, taking the comfort from her. Then she pulled back and wiped her face, glad she hadn't worn makeup to come help in the Mansion. "I haven't told my mom yet. She'll be so disappointed."

Lauren couldn't stomach the lecture either. And then she'd get a text with the suggestion to go see her therapist again, which actually wasn't a bad idea. But she didn't want it to come from her mom. She wanted her mother to hold her the way Aunt Mabel did and say what Aunt Mabel said.

"I'm sure it'll work out," she said.

Lauren gave her a look she hoped conveyed her disgust. "Really, Aunt Mabel? Is that what you thought about you and Kenneth?"

A pained look crossed her aunt's face. There one moment, and gone the next. And it had been almost sixty years since that relationship had ended. Lauren wondered if she'd be like that when she was in her eighties, still hurting over the loss of Trent Baker and his son.

Probably.

"Kenneth made his choice," Aunt Mabel said. "And it wasn't me. And not because I didn't try."

"Really?" Lauren said. "Seems like I heard a story at

Thanksgiving about how you told Gretchen not to let herself stand in her own way. That she'd always regret letting Andrew walk away from her."

"Well, everyone needs a push in the right direction." She lifted her head and patted her curls.

"So are you telling me you fought for Kenneth and he still left Hawthorne Harbor?" Lauren watched her aunt, the story not what she'd thought.

Sadness crept across her face, making her wrinkles deeper and showing her as much older than she'd just been. "Yes," she said quietly. "Which is fine. I did all I could." She looked at Lauren again, a bit of her old lady fire returning. "You have to be able to lie down at night and think you did all you could. So have you?"

The thought of seeing Trent again sent panic right through Lauren. "No," she said. "But I can't face him right now anyway." Besides, she hadn't done anything wrong.

"He probably feels as bad as you do," Mabel said, returning to the table settings. "Let's put Darrel and Kimmy here. Then your mom and dad. Then Eldon and Byron. They'll probably all like to sit together."

"What about those two spots back there?" She hadn't written down Trent's or Porter's name.

"Let's leave them for now," Aunt Mabel said, and Lauren wanted to argue. But she didn't. She also didn't pencil anyone in. She couldn't fathom a universe where Trent showed up to a massive Magleby family party when he didn't have to. Nope. Wasn't going to happen.

If only she could figure out what she'd done wrong, then she could apologize for it and try to get him back. But every time her mind went down this path, she couldn't think of anything.

It had been an *accident*. It could've happened while Trent slept in the bedroom beside his son's. Or while Betsy was sipping tea on the couch, waiting for Lauren to show up. Or while his nanny—whoever she was—dozed on the couch the way Lauren had been.

She hadn't freaked out at the sight of all the blood running down a little boy's face. She'd gotten a cloth wet and dabbed around until she found the wound. She had him hold a dry towel there while she cleaned up his foot enough to see the gash from the glass.

Then she'd carried him to her car and gotten him to the hospital, all while texting and calling his father. She hadn't missed a single step.

So why was Trent so angry with her?

Maybe she shouldn't have slammed the door on her way out...she'd apologize for that if she ever saw Trent Baker's handsome face again.

"Maybe in the new year you'd like to start learning how I've been running the Mansion," Aunt Mabel said, drawing Lauren out of her thoughts.

She got choked up again. "I would, Aunt Mabel."

Her aunt patted her arm and smiled, but it held a certain quality of melancholy that Lauren felt all the way through her soul.

"When do you want to retire?" she asked her aunt.

"Oh, when I'm dead." She added a laugh to the statement, and Lauren appreciated how she'd lightened the mood. But it only reminded her that Aunt Mabel would leave Hawthorne Harbor eventually too, and Lauren would once again be here on her own, trying to figure out who she was without her great aunt in her life.

LAUREN STILL HAD TRENT'S DECK TO FINISH. IT WOULD probably take two half-days to complete the railing, and she wanted to be paid the rest of her money. But she didn't want to be at his house when he was home, and since he was on the graveyard shift, he was home during the day. So she stuck to the basement and made good progress on it.

She remembered Trent telling her that he took quite a few days off over the Christmas holidays, because Porter didn't have school and he didn't like asking his family to babysit so much.

So she scheduled herself to finish his deck at the beginning of the first full week of January, hoping he wouldn't ask her about it.

Porter was another matter. She'd promised the boy while they were at the hospital that she'd take him for ice cream after everything was done. After the stitches and the shots. And she didn't break her promises to six-year-olds.

He must be so confused, she thought as she arrived at the house on the bluff. She paused overlooking the ocean, suddenly feeling very small and insignificant. She wondered how she'd feel if she had someone in her life one day, and then the next, they were gone.

Trent had lived through that when his wife died, and so had Porter, even if he was too young to remember it. And now that she and Trent weren't speaking, did Porter feel like he'd lost her?

Did he even care?

"Maybe he doesn't care," she said into the wind. But she cared, and she wanted to see him and let him know that just because she and his dad didn't get along anymore didn't mean she didn't like him.

So she finished up early that day and stopped by Duality to grab a couple of ice cream sandwiches. She was running a huge risk by going to the elementary school, but she didn't know where else to talk to Porter, and she couldn't go to his house. Trent would be there, and she knew he watched for Porter like a hawk. So he'd see them.

All she could do was pray he'd let her talk to him. It wasn't like she was a stalker or anything.

She parked in the lot and got out of her car, scanning the pick-up line. She didn't see Trent's truck or his police cruiser, so she positioned herself next to the fence and waited. More and more cars pulled into the circle drive, but she kept her eyes away from them.

The bell rang, and kids started pouring out of doors. It didn't take long for her to spot Porter, though it felt like hours. He walked with a crutch on his left side, supporting the foot he'd cut. He didn't wear a shoe on that foot, and she remembered the huge gash where his toes met his foot.

"Porter," she called, and he turned toward her. His face lit up, and she started toward him in the same moment he changed direction.

She crouched down in front of him, her stupid emotions threatening to spill out of her eyes again. "Hey, bud," she said, casting a quick glance over her shoulder to the pick-up line. "I promised you ice cream, and I didn't want to break my promise."

He looked at her with those brown eyes so like his father's and smiled. "Thanks, Lauren." He took the ice cream sandwich from her and then looked at her again. "Why aren't you staying with me anymore?"

So Trent hadn't told him. "Well, uh, that's a hard question to answer, Porty."

"I don't like Randi at all. She plays her music too loud, and it wakes me up."

"Porter." Trent's voice sent simultaneous shivers through Lauren's body, along with a healthy dose of adrenaline. She straightened and shaded her eyes as she looked back at him.

"I have to go," Lauren said. "I just didn't want to break my promise." She backed away from Porter, who hobbled badly now that he had a crutch and a backpack and an ice cream sandwich to juggle. She held up her hands, palms out, to Trent as if to say *I mean no harm.*

He simply watched her with that police officer mask in place, and she finally couldn't take it anymore. She turned and walked away, her head held high.

21

"She just gave me ice cream, Daddy," Porter said when Trent still hadn't moved. Almost all the kids had gone now, and still Trent couldn't get himself back to his truck. "It's good too. That Neapolitan kind from Duality you never let me get."

"Hm," Trent said, taking his son's crutch and sweeping the boy into his arms. The scent of sweat and sugar met his nose, and he suddenly wanted an ice cream sandwich too. "Why'd she bring you ice cream?"

He didn't want to admit that seeing Lauren Michaels crouched down in front of his son, and Porter's beaming face, had made his heart beat again. It hadn't been functioning properly since she'd left his house last Tuesday night.

It seemed impossible that it hadn't even been a week yet. He felt like she'd been gone forever.

"She said she would," Porter said simply. Trent opened the door and slid his son onto the seat.

"Buckle up, bud." He walked around the front of the truck and got in. "When did she say she would?"

"While we were in the hospital, before you got there. I had to get a big shot, and she said she'd buy me ice cream if I was really brave."

"Hm," Trent said again, but his mind wouldn't stop whirring. Savannah used to give Porter "shiny coins" if he did something she asked. She'd potty trained him with the promise of pennies and the candy they could buy, and Trent once again thought that Lauren would make a great mother.

So why hadn't he told her that on Tuesday night?

He'd been back over every detail of that night, and he was just as confused as ever. He kept coming back to his own guilt about having to leave Porter with anyone, and how he never wanted to get another phone call or text to come to the hospital for someone he loved.

So if you push Lauren away, you won't have to get that text, he thought.

And then his mind whispered, *Do you love Lauren?*

He wasn't sure what he felt, but he knew seeing her both hurt and thrilled him, and he knew he owed her an apology. And his gratitude.

After she'd walked out, he'd stayed in the kitchen for a few minutes, too stunned to move. Then he did go down the hall to the bathroom Porter used, and she had cleaned the whole thing. Not a speck of blood or glass or any evidence at all that an accident had taken place there existed—except in the big trash can beside his carport.

"Should've called her right then," he muttered, and Porter paused in his consumption of the ice cream sandwich.

"Who ya talkin' to, Daddy?"

"Just myself, bud." He flashed a fake smile and turned onto their street.

"Daddy, why isn't Lauren staying with me at night anymore?"

He pulled into the driveway and put the truck in park before he answered. "Did she ask you to ask me that?"

"No," Porter said, licking his fingers. "I asked her that, and she said it was a hard question to answer."

"Well, she's right."

"But you always tell me I can do hard things." He looked at Trent with such innocence, and Trent didn't want to disappoint him in any way.

"Well, you can."

"So what's the answer?"

Trent heaved a big breath. Because we got in a fight. Because I let myself push her away. Because I was worried about things becoming too serious with her. Because I love her.

He curled his fingers around the steering wheel and gripped it tightly. "You know I've been seeing her, right? Like, we're dating."

"Yeah, I know."

"Like, I kiss her and stuff, and we might get married."

Porter just blinked at him. "Really?" A smile spread across his whole face. "And then she can stay with me again while you work nights."

"Would you like that?"

"She's way better than Randi," Porter said, his grin fading. "She reads to me, and she was quiet."

His list for an acceptable mother seemed a bit short to Trent, but he chuckled. "I can talk to Randi about being quieter."

"But don't you like Lauren, Dad?"

He sighed. "Yeah, bud. I like her."

"She doesn't come over anymore."

"Yeah, that's because we broke up." The words hadn't been said, but he knew he was the one who needed to say a lot of things.

"Why'd you break up if you like her?"

Trent opened his door, the questions in Porter's child-like tone the same ones he'd been berating himself with for almost a week. And he still didn't have the answers. "That's a hard question to answer," he said.

"You can do hard things," Porter chirped just before Trent closed the door and then walked around to get his son out of the passenger side.

Inside, with Porter snacking away on a piece of toast and a banana, Trent pulled out his phone. Maybe he could get Lauren back over here by talking business.

When are you going to finish my deck?

He stared at the words and then deleted them. It sounded like a demand, and nothing ever translated well in texts or messages when feelings were already hurt. Trent knew that—wasn't that why he'd been called out last Tuesday in the first place?

Hurt feelings between a couple. Texts and messages that shouldn't have been sent.

She knew he had a deck that needed finishing, and he went out onto it to see what she had left to do. Just the railing, and the last conversation they'd had about it ran through his mind.

A couple more days, she'd said. Just a few hours. He looked back and forth between the unfinished railing and the pile of wood against his fence. There seemed like way more wood than was needed to finish the railing.

Maybe he could complete the deck for her...would that be like saying thank you?

He'd probably ruin the whole project. He knew how to prune rose bushes and lavender and make a hawthorn tree grow straight. But he knew nothing about construction.

But he knew someone who did. Or rather, someone who knew someone.

He dialed Jason Zimmerman, hoping he wouldn't have to give a big explanation to get a phone number. "Hey, man," Jason answered. "How's Porter?"

"Oh, he's doing great." Trent looked back into the house to make sure Porter didn't want to get down from the counter. He was still happily engrossed in the laptop, a piece of toast on the counter beside him.

"Hey, listen," Trent said. "I need to finish my deck. Your sister is dating Bennett Patterson, right? Do you have his number?"

"Yeah, sure I've got it. Just a sec." Jason went silent for a few seconds, then he asked, "I thought Lauren Michaels was doing it? Weren't you two getting serious?"

"Yeah," Trent said, hoping he could leave it at that.

"And she didn't finish?"

"Um, no."

"Hmm, that's good to know. I was going to hire her to do a gazebo for Kaitlyn. I swear its all my wife ever talks about. *This yard would look so great with a gazebo, right Jason?*" He laughed. "All right, I've got it. You ready?"

But Trent had frozen. He couldn't let Jason think Lauren had skipped out on finishing the deck. He couldn't cost her business in an attempt to make up with her.

"I don't need it," he said, making something up. He could lie in this situation, he was sure of it. "I just got a text from her. She's coming tomorrow."

"Oh, great," Jason said. "I'd love to come see the deck. I've heard she's the best general contractor in town."

"She is," Trent said. "You should definitely call her." He hung up and turned back to the house, at a complete loss for what to do now.

Just call her, came to mind, but he pushed it away. He'd *hurt* her—he could see that plainly on her face as she backed away from him. He hadn't liked that one bit, and he'd retreated behind a straight face so she wouldn't know the depth of his sorrow and guilt that he'd hurt her.

"Daddy, I want to get down."

He helped Porter down and over to the couch, and then he got busy in the kitchen making something for dinner, his mind stewing and bubbling the same way the pork and beans did as he stirred them.

By the time he spooned the beans over hot dogs and took a plate to Porter, he knew what he had to do.

He just didn't want to talk to Mabel Magleby about Lauren.

THE NEXT DAY, HE WOKE AT NOON AND GOT HIMSELF presentable to go up to the Mansion. He'd called Mabel last night and asked if he could meet with her that afternoon. She wanted to know what it was about, and she wouldn't let him off the phone until he'd blurted, "Lauren, okay? It's about Lauren."

His chest heaved now as it had last night, and he hadn't even left his house yet.

Mabel had said, "Wonderful. How about one o'clock? I'll have walnut cake ready."

And how could he say no to walnut cake?

His heart rate increased with every minute that ticked closer to one o'clock, and he felt sure his chest would explode before he actually made it to Mabel's cottage. But somehow, he did, and his legs took him right to the front door, too.

He knocked, and Mabel called, "It's open," from inside. He opened the door and went in just as Mabel came bustling out of the kitchen wearing an apron over her navy blue dress.

"Hello, Trent." She grinned at him like they got together for cake and tea every Tuesday at one o'clock, and she pulled him down into a hug. "It's good to see you."

He surveyed the dining room table, which was a far cry from the long table that had seated everyone for Thanksgiving. "That looks amazing," he said, remembering his manners. "I don't think I've ever had a walnut cake."

This cake had snow-white frosting swirled all over it, with candied walnuts along the outer edge. His mouth watered at the sight of it, and the scent of sugar and vanilla in the air.

She set a teapot on the table and then slid into a chair, leaving the other for him. He felt like a giant at a fairy tea table, but he forgot about all of that once she sliced into that cake and presented him with a piece.

"Miss Mabel," he said. "This looks almost sinful."

She grinned and cut herself a piece. Once she had her fork ready, they both dug in at the same time. He put his in his mouth, but she said, "So you're going to get back together with Lauren, right?"

He almost choked on the delectable cake, but he managed to keep it in his mouth and swallow it. It was nutty, and moist, and sweet, and the best cake he'd ever tasted. He nodded while he tried to get his voice to work.

"I messed up," he said, a bit sheepishly.

"You certainly did."

"Did she tell you what happened?"

She pointed her forkful of cake at him, her eyes sharp and missing nothing. "She said you didn't think she'd be a good mother, and then she said she'd been stupid. Then there were too many tears after that." She put the cake in her mouth, and she did *not* look happy to be eating it, though Trent knew it was *him* she was not happy with.

Join the club, he thought.

"So what do I do?" he asked. "People make mistakes, you know."

"Well, do you think she'll be a good mother to Porter?"

"Yes," Trent said quietly. "He loves her, and she said she loves him."

"Mm." Mabel ate more cake, but Trent had lost his sweet tooth. He waited for her to say something else, but she just sat there.

"So I'm guessing you're going to make me figure this out on my own?" he asked.

She looked at him with the same puppy dog eyes his son always did. Trent laughed and shook his head. "I don't know what to do."

"Sure you do. You know her whole family is coming to

town this weekend. You know where a florist is. You know where to buy a ring. You know where she'll be, and what time she'll be there. Get it done."

Trent blinked at her. "Are you suggesting what I think you're suggesting?"

"I didn't suggest anything." Mabel lifted her chin and took another bite of cake. "Now are you going to eat that, or go get a few *errands* done today?"

He looked from the cake to her. Then he picked up his plate, and said, "Both," and took another bite of the heavenly walnut cake on his way out the door.

22

Lauren lit the pine tree scented candle on Saturday morning, about the same time her parents should've been leaving Seattle. She still hadn't told them about Trent, not being able to bring herself to say the words out loud to her mother.

She hadn't even really said anything to Aunt Mabel. The crying said plenty, but she was determined not to cry today. Her parents hadn't visited Hawthorne Harbor in a couple of years, and she was going to take them to lunch and they were going to spend the day shopping and talking and enjoying one another's company.

Her brothers would be here tomorrow, and Aunt Mabel was hosting Christmas Eve at her cottage, where her parents and Kimmy were staying. Lauren's brothers would bunk with her for a couple of nights, and Lauren was thrilled everyone would be in town for a few days.

She didn't need Trent. In fact, he'd probably be a distraction, and she'd have to check with him all the time to make sure he stayed happy.

Without him, all she had to worry about was herself. It was a depressing and freeing thought, and she couldn't make heads nor tails of it.

She focused on cleaning up the house. She wasn't exactly a slob, but her top priority wasn't dusting or making sure the windowsills got wiped. But that morning, as the candle filled the house with the scent of Christmas trees, she got her house into tip-top shape.

The guest bedrooms were ready, the dishwasher hummed with her week's dishes, and she'd even put fresh towels in both bathrooms.

She took a deep breath and took off her cleaning apron. With all the supplies back in the linen closet, she pulled her hair out of its ponytail and started a pot of coffee. Her father drank the stuff all day and all night, and he still slept like the dead.

"Hello?"

Lauren teared up at the sound of her mother's voice, and she practically skipped down the hall and into the foyer where her parents stood. "Mom. Dad." She launched herself at them, and they both hugged her at the same time.

At least these tears weren't because of Trent, and she wasn't embarrassed by them. "How was the drive? Is it raining again?"

Lauren was wholeheartedly tired of the rain, but the ruckus outside indicated Mother Nature didn't care how she felt.

"Started about an hour ago," her dad said.

"Your tree is wonderful." Her mom stepped over to the short six-footer and touched one of the gingerbread man ornaments.

"Thanks, I bought it at the Festival of Trees."

"Are they still doing that?" Her mom glanced around the house as if she'd never been there.

"Yep," Lauren said. "Every year." She'd told her mom that she made all the tree stands, but she didn't say it again.

"I love this house," her mom said, facing her with a smile. Her own dark hair had started to get streaked with gray, and she had a few more wrinkles than Lauren remembered. She glanced at her dad, who wore a jacket with a salmon over his heart, and he definitely looked older than the picture in her mind.

"Did you know this was going to be my place?" Her mom ran her fingers along the shelf Lauren had installed above the fireplace.

"I didn't know that," Lauren said. "I mean, I knew it was Magleby family property. I didn't know they'd been assigned to people." She'd lived in the house in the six years since she'd been back in town, after her disastrous relationship with Rick.

"Oh, yes," her mother said. "Everyone has certain land

and property." Her smile slipped a little, and she tugged on the ends of her sweater sleeves.

"I love your sweater, Mom," Lauren said. The hunter green looked good with her mom's complexion, and the silver Christmas trees were the perfect amount of festive.

"Hmm? Thanks." She was very distracted today, and Lauren thought she might be able to get away with making an excuse for Trent and moving on. On Christmas Day, there would be so many people at the Mansion, surely she could get away with sitting beside her single brothers without having to answer a million questions.

But she couldn't lie. If either of her parents asked about Trent, she'd have to say they'd broken up. If that indeed was what had happened. Neither of them had ever said those words, but neither of them were saying anything at the moment.

"So, when do we get to meet Trent?" her mother asked, and Lauren's stomach wrapped around itself.

"Well, not today," Lauren said as brightly as she could. "It didn't work out."

Concern entered her mother's eyes instantly. "You two broke up? When?" She cut a quick glance at Lauren's dad.

"Oh, a couple of weeks ago," Lauren said like it was no big deal, like she hadn't been staring out the window at the rain every evening until she was too tired to think, like she hadn't been crying daily. "He's probably gone out to Bell Hill for the weekend."

"What happened?" Her mom stepped over to her and

took both of her hands in hers. "You liked him, didn't you?'

"I did." Lauren pressed her lips together to keep her emotions in check. "I just think I'm a little too different from his first wife." She hadn't even known she thought that, but it felt right.

"Was it the little boy?" Her mom looked right into Lauren's eyes.

"Megan," Lauren's dad said, a heavy dose of warning in his voice.

"It wasn't Porter," Lauren said. "I really liked him too. We got along great." A nostalgic feeling wafted over her and she gave her mom a quick smile. "Now, what I'm ready for now is lunch. My friend Gillian is going to meet us."

Lauren made her family-famous chocolate mousse pie early in the morning on Christmas Eve. It needed time to set in the fridge, and this way she wouldn't have to be busy in the kitchen while her brothers were here.

They arrived in a flurry of voices and hugs, and Lauren's happiness shot off the charts.

"Nice beard," she said to Eldon with a giggle. "Is that what they're wearing in Seattle these days?"

"At the video game company," Darrel said, rubbing his smooth jaw.

"You wish you could grow a beard like this," Eldon said, supremely confident.

"Nah," Darrel said with a smile. "Then Kimmy wouldn't kiss me." His eyes twinkled, and Kimmy turned from the old family photo Lauren kept on the same shelf her mom had admired the day before.

"Did you say my name?" she asked, moving back over to the group.

"Nope." Darrel put his arm around her and brought her close to him. Lauren couldn't help watching their interactions, the way Kimmy looked at him with stars in her eyes. Did she look at Trent like that?

Byron returned from putting his bags in the bedroom where he'd be staying. "Lauren, can you cut my hair?"

He was wearing quite the mop on top of his head, and Lauren went into the hall he'd just come down. "I think I can. I haven't cut anyone's hair in a while." She got out her clippers and drape, somewhat surprised she still had them. But her mother had taught her how to cut hair when she was only twelve years old, and she'd been making her brothers look more presentable for decades now.

"Sit here." She moved a barstool away from the counter and snapped the drape around his neck.

"So Mom says you broke up with Trent," Darrel said, apparently moving into the serious part of the conversation.

"I didn't," Lauren said. "It was a mutual agreement."

Byron scoffed. "Do those exist?"

"Sure they do," Lauren said, plugging in the clippers. "And I have scissors in my hand, so you better be careful what you say."

"Short on the sides," he said. "Don't make me look bald on top."

She ran her fingers through his hair. "Uh, Byron, you're already going bald on top."

"I know," he said, swatting her hand away. "So not too short up there, okay?"

She grinned at her other brothers, who didn't seem to have any problems with their hair and started buzzing Byron's head. "So tell me all about Seattle," she said. "Sometimes I really miss it."

"It's just different from here," Byron said.

"Bigger," Darrel said. "Sometimes I think you're the one who's got things figured out, Lauren. Small town. People who care about you."

She kept cutting Byron's hair, but her mind tried to find someone who cared about her in Hawthorne Harbor. Gillian, for sure. Aunt Mabel. Maybe Uncle Mitch, and Gene, and Kam. But everyone else? Would they even know if she closed up Michaels Construction and took it somewhere it?

"Maybe you should meet my friend Gillian," she said. "She's pretty, and she's a real estate agent, so she can relocate."

Byron laughed. "I'm not letting my older sister set me up."

"Why not?"

"I'm just not."

"He doesn't date," Eldon said from the couch. "He keeps waiting for Michelle to decide he's the one."

"I am not," Byron said, but he wasn't very convincing. Lauren loved the relationship her brothers had, and while she hadn't been around them for a while, she still fit right in.

"Michelle?" she asked. "Didn't you guys break up like, two years ago?"

"Twenty-six months," Eldon said over the noise of the clippers.

"It's fine," Byron said, and Lauren felt him watching her. So she didn't say anything else. She certainly wouldn't want her brothers bugging her about Trent.

They spent the day laughing at lunch, and walking through the Christmas shops, and watching the sun shine weakly over the ocean. When they arrived at Aunt Mabel's, the house smelled like ham and coffee, two of Lauren's favorite things.

Her parents both helped in the kitchen, and Aunt Mabel greeted Lauren's brothers with open arms and smiles. It was loud and festive, and Lauren stood back and admired her great aunt's tree, and the spread of delicious foods on the counter, and her family. Her whole family.

"What are you smiling about?" Aunt Mabel asked, her

jolly demeanor fading. "Come help me set the table." She nodded to a stack of plates, and Lauren laughed as she picked them up. She moved around the table—smaller than the one at Thanksgiving, but bigger than the one she'd seen in Mabel's house before.

"Aunt Mabel," she said. "There are only eight of us." And yes, she still held two plates.

"We need those," she said, completely nonplussed.

"We do?" Lauren tried to meet her eye. "For who?"

"I invited a couple of people who didn't have anywhere else to go." She kept her back to Lauren as she gathered the napkins.

Lauren's heart leapt, but she reasoned that it couldn't be Trent. He had his whole family in town, and surely he'd made plans with them for the holidays. She laid out utensils, the napkins, and started filling glasses with ice.

With whisking and steam rising from the stovetop, dinner came together, and Aunt Mabel clapped her hands a few times. Lauren had seen her do the same with her staff when she wanted to make an announcement, and she grinned as her family settled down the same way Aunt Mabel's employees did.

"I'm so glad Lauren invited you all for the holidays," Aunt Mabel said, glowing the same way she had at the unveiling. "I know we're having a giant family dinner tomorrow for Christmas, but I'm so grateful we're doing this smaller affair. Now, Paul will you say grace?"

Her father nodded, and bowed his head. Lauren let

her dad's words roll over her, feeling peaceful and grateful for her family too. With the prayer over, everyone started taking plates from the table and moving back over to the bar to dish up what they wanted to eat.

Aunt Mabel's guests still hadn't arrived, so Lauren left the two plates beside each other and took the only one left, standing back and basking in the energy of her family. She'd never appreciated them growing up, especially being the oldest and having to babysit her rambunctious younger brothers all the time.

But she sure did love them now.

Darrel returned to the line after going to his seat, so he stood between her and the front door when someone knocked.

"Oh, they're here," Aunt Mabel said, really moving quickly for a woman her age. She opened the door and stood there. Lauren spooned more creamed corn onto her plate and listened for a voice. Maybe then she'd be able to recognize these special guests of Aunt Mabel's.

But she couldn't hear them over Eldon's laughter. So it wasn't until Aunt Mabel clapped again and said, "Everyone. These are my friends, Trent and Porter," that Lauren looked toward the front door.

Her heart seized, as did all of her muscles.

No.

Aunt Mabel would not invite them without telling Lauren.

But she obviously had, as Trent, in all his police officer glory, and Porter entered the cottage.

A hush had fallen over the house, so that when Lauren dropped her plate, it landed with an ear-splitting *crash!*

23

Trent fought the urge to reach up and adjust the tie he wore. Aunt Mabel hadn't ever come out and said anything that would help him know what to do. But he'd learned that if he asked the right questions, she'd say, "I would."

So he wore black slacks and a pale yellow shirt, complete with a necktie as if he were going to church. He'd taken care to make sure Porter looked festive and handsome as well, thanks to Eliza. She'd come through in a pinch and taken Porter shopping for pants that weren't made of denim and didn't have rips in them.

She'd talked to him about what was happening with Trent and Lauren, and he'd shown her the ring he'd purchased for the woman currently staring at him with horror running through her eyes.

He swallowed, thinking this surprise visit to be a very bad idea. But Mabel had insisted it would be romantic, and big, and exactly what Trent needed to do to make things right between him and Lauren.

His eyes traveled from her to the people sitting at the table, all of whom stared as if they'd never seen a man with brown hair before. The ring in his pocket felt like a piece of lead, and he released the fingers he'd curled into a fist and lifted his hand into a wave.

"Hello, everyone," he said, his voice a bit shaky. "I'm Trent, and this is my son, Porter."

"Lauren's Trent?" her mother asked, partially rising from her place at the table. Her gaze darted to her daughter. "I thought you two broke up."

"Yes, well, the man recognizes the error of his ways," Mabel said, nudging Trent forward and out of the doorway. "Don't you, Trent?"

"Yes," he said, stumbling forward a few steps.

"Go on," she said. "Get some food."

Lauren flew into motion then, cleaning up her fallen plate and the food that had scattered. Trent stepped over to where she stood in the kitchen, his nerves almost paralyzing him. But he pushed past it and said, "Hey, Lauren."

Her eyes flew to his, and the nervousness there made his heart ache. "I'm sorry," he said. "I'm going to say that first." He swallowed again, his stomach tight and his muscles tighter. "I'm really sorry for acting like such a jerk when Porter got hurt."

She glanced at Porter, who'd come with Trent, really quite good with his crutch now. He didn't even really need it anymore, but he still couldn't wear a shoe without too much pain, so he brought the crutch just in case.

When she looked back at Trent, she said, "You really were a jerk."

"I know," he said. "And I've wanted to say thank you for a couple of weeks now too. You really took great care of Porter that night, and cleaned up the bathroom, and... thank you."

Her expression softened, and Trent was very aware of her family sitting only feet away from where they stood.

The speech he'd prepared and practiced was nowhere to be found in his mind, and he realized he was going to have to wing it.

"I'm not great with words," he said.

"Oh, you're doing great," someone said, and Trent looked over to the table as a few people chuckled. Lauren's brothers were watching her, and he felt like he should be worried about impressing them. But they all wore a smile on their face, and Trent realized it was her mother he was going to have to win over.

He looked back to Lauren. "I'm really not great at saying how I feel." He licked his lips and glanced at Porter.

"Just tell her, Dad."

"I love you," he blurted, his heart racing around inside his chest like it was trying to find the finish line. "I love you, and I'm hoping you'll find some way to forgive me so we can try again."

He took a deep breath, because he felt like he was about to pass out. "I think that's all. I mean, obviously, I had it all rehearsed and it sounded so much better than that."

"And that's not all," Mabel said.

Trent looked at her, almost wanting to tell her he'd had enough of her nudging. One could call it meddling.

"Yes, it is," he said. "For now." He faced Lauren again, and while he'd thought about this moment for several days now, it was much worse having to live it.

She stared back at him, and he had no idea what else to say.

"Lauren," Porter said, and she bent down until she was eye-level with him.

"Yeah, bud?"

"I promise he'll be nicer."

She leaned her forehead against Porter's, a smile touching her face and making her shine like gold. Trent wanted her to smile at him like that, and he watched the sweet moment between her and his son.

"And we don't break our promises, do we?" she asked.

Porter shook his head, and Lauren straightened and met Trent's eye again. "All right," she said.

"All right?" Trent repeated. "All right what?"

She sighed like he was making her life difficult on

purpose, and then she giggled. "I suppose we can try again, because I kinda like you too."

"Is that so?" he asked, relief painting his insides.

"Yeah." She stepped closer, her eyes dropping to his mouth. "In fact, I'm in love with you too."

Trent had never heard better words, and he drew her into an embrace. She felt so good in his arms, and a sigh passed through his whole body. "Can I kiss you in front of your family?" he whispered in her ear. This public reconciliation wasn't really his scene, and he'd never done it before.

"I think there might be a riot if you don't."

So Trent cradled her face in his hands and lowered his mouth to hers. Kissing her was just as wonderful as it always had been, and as her family clapped and whooped, Trent thanked his lucky stars that he'd listened to Mabel Magleby.

Lauren pulled away, giggling, sooner than Trent would've liked, but he reminded himself he wasn't alone with her. Heat flamed in his face as she said, "So these are my brothers. Darrel, Eldon, and Byron."

They stood and Trent shook hands with all of them. "And you're all younger, right?"

"That's right," Eldon, the one with the big beard, said. "Lauren likes to lord her age over us."

Trent laughed, though he didn't know Lauren to lord anything over anyone.

"And my parents," Lauren said, edging past her brothers. "Oh, this is Kimmy, Darrel's girlfriend."

"Nice to meet you," Trent said, nodding at the blonde woman. He'd been planning to meet Lauren's parents yesterday, and he told himself one day late wasn't too bad.

"This is my dad, Paul." Lauren stood beside him and faced Trent. She wore a bit of nervousness in her dark eyes. "And my mom, Megan."

"Sir." Trent shook her dad's hand, hoping he'd made a good first impression. He was dressed nicely, and Porter was behaving. That had to count for something, right? "Ma'am." He saw Lauren's feminine features in her mom's face, though her hair was lighter, shorter, and thinner. She also didn't have quite the same eyes, but the slope of her nose was Lauren's.

Lauren joined him at his side. "This is Trent Baker, the man I've been telling you about."

"Police officer," Paul said. "Right?"

"Right," he said. "I train the K9 dogs, and other stuff."

"He wants to be a full-time canine trainer," Lauren said, slipping her hand through his arm, which grounded him.

"Well, that's just a dream," he said, cutting her a glance. "And with Lauren's general contracting business and stuff here, I don't know...." His voice trailed off, and he forced himself to swallow.

Megan gaped at him. "So you would consider Lauren's—?"

"Mom," Lauren said sharply, and her mom switched her gaze to her daughter's.

"What?"

"He's not Rick," she said quietly, her chin dropping a little. Trent wanted to lift her up, support her, until she didn't speak with such shame in her voice.

Megan looked at Trent again, but he kept his eyes on Lauren. "You okay?" he asked softly, his lips barely moving.

Lauren looked at him, and oh, how Trent wanted to be alone with her. *Soon*, he told himself. *Soon.*

She nodded and that fire that he loved so much re-entered her eyes. She faced her mom again. "Yes, Mom, Trent would consider my company, my feelings, my everything, before he made a decision that would impact us all." She twisted a waved at Porter to come join them. "And Porter too. We have to consider him in everything we do." She hugged him to her side, and if Trent had any doubts about loving her—which he didn't—that simple action and those powerful words would've erased them.

Her mom pressed her lips together and nodded, brushing at her eyes quickly. She stepped up to Lauren and hugged her, saying, "I'm so happy for you."

"Yes, yes," Mabel said. "Everything is hunky dory. Can we eat before Eldon snitches all the ham?"

Trent started to chuckle, but the sound got stuck in his throat when Megan grabbed onto him too, and said, "Thank you for loving her for who she is."

AN HOUR LATER, WHILE MABEL BREWED COFFEE AND PUT Megan to work whipping cream for the pies, Trent managed to sneak out the front door with Lauren. He didn't really sneak. He had to make sure Porter would be taken care of, but all that took was a look at Lauren's dad, and he said, "Porter, want me to show you how I taught Lauren to build a flower box?"

"Your parents are wonderful," he said, securing his hand in hers. "I like them."

"They like you too." She squeezed his fingers. "You really know how to make a scene, don't you?"

"Is that what that was?" He laughed, the sound flying away into the huge sky above them. At least it wasn't raining anymore, but it certainly was a gray day. He touched the engagement ring in his pocket, wondering if he should save it for another time.

"I think so," she said. "But I appreciate the apology."

"I...don't know what happened that night," he said. "There were a lot of confusing things happening in the days leading up to it, and I just think something snapped in my brain." The part that knew how to reason.

"It's okay," she said. "I've lost my head a time or two in my life."

"Well, from now on, we'll have to keep each other in check."

"Deal." She danced in front of him as the crested the hill and the Mansion appeared before them. "So I have a Christmas present for you and Porter, but you're not going to get it for a couple of weeks." Her eyes sparkled like glimmering candles, and Trent wanted to wrap his arms around her and spin her around until they were both dizzy.

Trent's eyebrows went up as he smiled. "Why's that?"

"And you can't go in your back yard until I say you can."

"But the dogs are back there."

"I'll get them for you."

"You'll be at my house in the morning?"

Lauren's excitement visibly dimmed. "Yeah, that's not going to work, is it?" She glanced away, down the hill toward her house. "Do you think we have time to stop by my place?"

"I don't have anything else to do today, and I think your parents will keep Porter for a while." He hadn't said anything to his son, but Porter was quite good at entertaining those he was with.

"Okay, then I'll show you the gift."

"You can show it to me?"

"Yeah." She started down the hill, the brown grass crunching under her feet.

"But I thought it was going to be in my back yard." Confusion pulled through him as he hurried to catch her.

When he strode alongside her, she said, "It is. You'll see," and steadfastly refused to answer any more of his questions. With every step, he wondered if he could show her his gift too, and his fingers tightened around the diamond one more time.

24

L
auren's stomach vibrated with jitters. She'd felt this way a couple of times in her life, and nothing had ever worked out all the well afterward. But she didn't want Trent to think she'd abandoned his deck, or that she hadn't gotten him anything for Christmas.

So she ignored his questions as they took the walk down to her house. It was farther than it looked, and by the time they arrived, Lauren knew she wouldn't want to walk back up the hill. She could take the work truck up and get one of her brothers to drive it back down.

"Okay, so you wait here," she said when they stood in her kitchen.

"Can I get a drink?"

"Sure, get me one too." Lauren dashed down the hall to her office without another word. The plans for Trent's deck sat beneath a stack of folders, and she pulled them out and smoothed them over the surface of the desk.

She'd bought enough wood to make the pergola, but she'd never mentioned it to him. She'd calculated her time, and she knew she'd be able to get the project done before Christmas, wrap a big red bow around the post, and say, "Ta-da!" before the big day.

Well, she'd had those plans before they'd broken up. Now, the deck wouldn't even be finished in time for Christmas—and Trent had never said a word about it. He hadn't texted her, asking when she'd finish the deck. Nothing.

Breathing deeply, she took the plans down the hall and into the kitchen. "So." She laid them out on the table. "This is the deck you ordered." She pointed to the lines, the width of it. "I only need a couple of half-days of work to get the railings done. But." She pulled the top paper off the stack to reveal the drawing underneath.

"I want to give you this."

Trent sucked in a breath and asked, "What is this?" He ran his fingertip down the diagonal line of the pergola's roof. "Is this...what is this?"

Lauren looked at her design with fondness, imagining it in Trent's back yard. It would be perfect. "It's a pergola," she said. "They'd normally meant as a type of patio cover, but they're open. But I designed this one with clear panes in the top so the light comes through but the rain stays out."

Trent stared at the drawings. "It does rain a lot in Washington."

"So these pillars attach to the railing, and you can put in windows eventually, if you wanted to convert the deck to an outdoor room. Or we can tie curtains on the openings. You could put Christmas lights along the wood too, and it would be an fantastic place to sit in the evenings."

Lauren herself wanted this pergola. "It'll take another few weeks to build," she said. "I already have all the wood. I've ordered the panels, but they got delayed out of British Columbia."

He moved and put his arm around her, and she leaned into the strength of his body.

"The roof is slanted," she said. "But it won't ruin your view of the yard. And...." She reached for the corner of the paper. "The design includes two hammocks. One for you and one for Porter."

"Lauren," he whispered, her name full of emotion. "This is too much."

"It's what that back yard needs."

Trent simply stared at the page for another few moments. "You'll have to let me pay for it."

"Then it wouldn't be a gift." Lauren turned into him and looked up at him. He gazed back at her with equal adoration as she felt moving through her. "I want you to have the perfect back yard."

He bent down and touched his lips to hers quickly.

"Okay, so I have something to show you, and it might influence these plans." He nodded toward the table.

"Oh?" Lauren couldn't think of a single thing that would make her not want to build this pergola for Trent and Porter.

He stepped back and dug his hand into his pocket. He withdrew it slowly to reveal a modest diamond pinched between his thumb and forefinger.

Lauren gasped and covered her mouth with both hands. "Trent," she said, the sound muffled. She couldn't look away from the sparkling gem.

"I was thinking you and I should get married," he said. "Wait. Wait, wait, wait. That's not how this is supposed to go." He dropped to one knee and held the ring up as if she hadn't seen it properly.

"I love you, Lauren Michaels, and I want you to be my wife and Porter's mother. I will do my best to make you happy every day of my life. Will you marry me?"

Pure shock poured through her. How long had he had that ring? Had it been in his pocket for weeks?

"So you have a hard floor," he said, and Lauren startled.

"Oh, I—"

"Too soon?" he asked, his face falling a little.

Lauren moved then, practically lunging at him and bypassing the ring. She took his face into her hands, and said, "Definitely not too soon." She kissed him, wondering if this love flowing between them would always be so thrilling.

"So is that a yes?" he asked, his lips catching on hers and jumbling his question.

"Yes," she said, kissing him again. "Yes, that's a yes."

He grinned, stood, and slipped the ring on her finger. "See how this affects your beautiful deck and pergola?"

"Not really," she said.

"Well." He touched the plans again. "I don't see us living in my house. You're going to take over the Mansion one day, and your place here is bigger than mine, and actually a lot nicer, and I thought we'd live here."

The way he ducked his head was adorable, and Lauren couldn't wait to share her life with him. "And I don't have a house payment," she said.

He jerked his attention to her. "You own this place?"

"It's been in the family for generations," she said. "So yeah. I own it."

"Well, we're definitely living here then." He laughed and tucked her against his chest. "Or wherever you want. I honestly don't care, as long as we're together."

And those were the best words Lauren had ever heard.

A FEW DAYS LATER, LAUREN WORKED IN TRENT'S YARD. SHE hadn't given up on the pergola idea, but she saw his point about not investing the money and time into a deck he'd only enjoy for a few months.

Okay, almost a year, as she'd always wanted a fall wedding. She'd sat down with her mother on Christmas morning, before the big Magleby family dinner, and they'd put September tenth on the calendar.

Lauren had enjoyed exactly two days of her engagement secret, and then she'd told Gillian. After all, she'd need help with the dress, the shoes, the flowers, the decorations, all of it.

But Aunt Mabel would take care of a lot of that. After all, the wedding would be at the Mansion, and she'd already insisted on a full three-course meal as part of the ceremony.

Lauren wanted to give Trent and Porter the deck anyway. Plus, it would increase the resell value of his home. So she measured and cut, nailed and sanded.

By the new year, the hammocks were ready to go in, and she prohibited Porter and Trent from coming into the back yard until she had them installed. The wind blew, but even if it rained, she wouldn't get wet, because the clear panels had come in and they were beautiful.

She finished and stood back, her back aching but the sight before her absolutely worth it. After stepping over to the door, she opened it and called, "You guys want to come see?"

"I do!" Porter's little boy footsteps ran toward her, and she stepped back so she wouldn't get trampled. A dog barked, and then claws slipped on the hard floor as all four dogs followed him.

Trent said something, appearing behind the dogs. He barked a command at them again, and they all stopped. Wilson, the pack leader, whined, and Trent shushed him. He stepped to their side and then in front of them and let them come with him.

She wanted to see their faces, but she stood beside them instead.

"Wow," Porter said.

"Go try it out," Lauren said. "They're good for up to five hundred pounds, so you could all get in the same one."

Porter moved forward and got in the blue and white striped hammock. "This is great," he said. "Come lay down, Daddy."

Trent looked at Lauren and said, "You're amazing," before joining his son in the hammock. He yipped at the dogs, and they trotted over, eager to please him. They struggled to get in, especially with all three humans laughing, and Lauren snapped a picture of the six of them in one hammock.

Then Porter pushed the dogs out and they went down the steps to the yard. He moved over to the other hammock, and Trent motioned for Lauren to come join him.

So she did, cuddling easily into his side and sighing. "Merry Christmas," she said, and he chuckled.

NINE MONTHS LATER

Trent had watched Lauren over the past several months as she tried to keep up with Michaels Construction and learn how to run the events at the Mansion. Sometimes he and Porter went up to the grounds and hung out while she walked around with Mabel, taking notes.

She was exhausted most of the time, and Trent didn't blame her. She always made time for him and Porter, and she'd encouraged him to pursue the idea of training canine dogs full-time.

"So we're getting married tomorrow," he said to her when he arrived at the Mansion on September ninth.

She grinned. "We sure are."

"You have everything ready?"

"Yes," she said. "My parents are coming tonight sometime. Gillian is picking up the dress and staying with me tonight." She straightened from where she was putting towels in a low cabinet.

"Anything I can do to help?" He wrapped his arms around her and hugged her, still somewhat in shock that she was about to be his. He'd had several moments of self-doubt over the months, but as soon as he saw Lauren again, they went away. She didn't seem to feel like she was second-best or that she wasn't equal to the task of raising Porter.

"Nope," she said. "Well, show up." She laughed, and he smiled too. "And bring the dogs early. Your dad will have their bow ties."

A hint of sadness touched his heart. "Only two," he murmured.

"How are Wilson and Brutus doing?"

"Great, last I heard," he said. They'd both been taken on with the Chicago Police Department as narcotics dogs over the summer, and he'd gotten a few pictures as the weeks went by.

And he wasn't the only one who missed the two dogs. Tornado and Pecorino barely knew what to do with themselves, and he hoped they'd behave during the wedding tomorrow.

"Any leads on a new dog?"

"No." He sighed. "I thought Ruthie would work out, but she gave up on that ball after twenty minutes." And police dogs didn't give up, ever. They worked until they accomplished their tasks. "I think I'm going to adopt her anyway."

Lauren wiped her hair out of her face. "I knew you would."

"You okay with that?"

"Of course. You can have as many dogs as you want." She squeezed past him and walked toward the kitchen.

"That's why I love you," he said, following her. "I got the dog run in your back yard done." He also had one more thing to tell her, but he wanted it to be a surprise. He reasoned that it would be a surprise no matter when he told her.

"Hey," he said, catching her hand before she went into the kitchen. "I know you're checking on stuff for tomorrow, and I promise I'm going to get out of your hair."

"You're not bothering me." She looked up at him. "Okay, what's going on?"

She knew him so well, and Trent really liked that. "I think I do want to quit at the department and train dogs full-time."

Instead of frowning and questioning him about how they could pay their bills, she grinned and said, "Good idea. And you'll take Mabel's offer?"

Trent nodded, having thought about being the manager at the Mansion for a month before the idea had really sunk in. "Yes, I think so. The dogs I'm training can come up here. They'll have access to people and situations, and Adam said I could still use the police supplies."

"You've talked to him already?"

"Briefly," Trent said, glancing at Jaime as he came in from outside. He'd never seen himself as a property and event manager, but Mabel was really getting up there in age, and she wanted the Mansion to stay in the family.

Lauren would be the new owner of the Mansion, but she wanted to keep doing her construction business as well. So while she'd been learning the ropes at the Mansion for the past nine months, she didn't want to run the operations of the place on a day-to-day basis.

So Trent would.

"There you are," Mabel said as she stepped out of the kitchen. "Come taste this sauce. You're going to love it." She looked from Lauren to Trent. "Oh, dear. What did I interrupt?"

Lauren patted Trent's chest and looked at her great aunt. "Trent's going to take the manager job and train dogs."

"Of course he is." Mabel looked irritable, like this decision should've been made ages ago. And maybe it should've. But Trent did like to take his time on life decisions, as they affected a lot more than just him.

"Of course he is," Lauren mimicked, giving her great aunt a kiss on the cheek as she moved into the kitchen. "Now, where's this sauce?"

∾

TRENT WOKE on his wedding day, his heart booming around inside his chest like someone was beating it with a big mallet. He hadn't wanted to make a big deal out of the wedding, but it was Lauren's first ceremony, and she was well-known in Hawthorne Harbor. Or at least the Magleby's were, and everyone within a hundred-mile radius knew she was set to inherit the Magleby Mansion once Mabel died.

But Mabel just kept kicking, and Trent suspected she had many more years at the Mansion and around town.

Lauren had asked his sister to help her, so Trent was left to his own devices to get himself and Porter up to the Mansion. He texted Eliza when he got there to make sure Lauren was safely hidden away in the west wing she'd redesigned.

With the coast clear, he took Porter up the steps and to the right instead of the left. The groom's rooms were much less impressive than the brides, but he had plenty of space to get dressed and comb his hair. Porter too. They were ready in only a half an hour, and he looked out the window at the outdoor area where they'd be married.

Dozens of chairs had been set up, and Jaime worked with three other men to put up a big white tent. Colored streamers got hung on the corners, and someone knocked on the door to his suite.

"Yeah," he said, and his parents came in. His mother carried the flowers for him and Porter and she wept as she pinned them on.

"Mom," he said, not sure what else to say to comfort her.

"They're happy tears," she said. "I'm just so glad you found someone again." She sniffled. "You two are just so handsome. She is so lucky to have you."

"I think we're the lucky ones, Mom." Trent glanced at Porter. "Right, bud?"

Porter shrugged, which caused everyone to laugh, and then his mom took his hand. "Come on, buddy. You're coming with me for a few minutes." She glanced at Trent. "Your dad has the bow ties for the dogs and then Mabel wants the three of you downstairs."

"I'm okay to leave?"

"Yep, as long as you can get down there in the next ten minutes."

His dad handed him the two bow ties for Tornado and Pecorino, and his parents left with Porter.

"All right, guys," he said to the dogs. "Come get dressed." The dogs didn't know that command, and he grinned at them as he bent down and got their bows onto their collars. "No barking, okay? This isn't about you."

He barely thought it was about him. No, he'd been married before, and he knew this wedding was all about Lauren.

He made it downstairs and into position inside the timeframe Mabel had given him, and he was surprised to see that the chairs were nearly full of people. And more and more just kept coming.

It felt like a long time but was really only a few minutes before Mabel signaled him and he got up from where he'd been sitting with his family. He stood by the altar, calling both dogs over with him.

He turned to see his son standing in the doorway, his hands held just so. A moment later, he started walking, but it wasn't a normal stride. Trent chuckled at the formality of it, and he grinned as his son started down the aisle, carrying a pink rose.

Porter stood next to him while the rest of the wedding party marched down the aisle, and then finally—*finally*—Lauren appeared.

Her dress was pure white and gorgeous, rising and swelling along her curves. The bottom half was miles and miles of ruffled fabric, and Trent could barely breathe as she walked toward him, a rosy blush in her cheeks.

Porter stepped forward and handed her the rose, and she bent down to hug him. When she straightened and Trent took her hand in his, he caught the hint of tears in her eyes. It warmed his heart to see how much she loved his son, and together they faced the pastor.

He hoped they would face everything together.

The pastor had been instructed not to speak for too long, so before Trent knew it, it was time to say I do.

Lauren did first, and then Trent gazed at her as he said, "I do."

"You may kiss your bride."

Trent felt every emotion in the book in that moment,

but the greatest of them all was joy. He kissed Lauren—his wife—and whispered, "I love you."

"I love you too," she said back, then she turned toward the crowd and lifted their joined hands.

Hawthorne Harbor
SECOND CHANCE ROMANCE
the end

SNEAK PEEK! THE DAY HE CAME HOME
CHAPTER ONE

H unter Magleby watched the ocean on his left-hand side, his heart slowly sinking toward his feet with every mile that passed. Well, the left one at least could still feel something. His right foot ached with a numbness the doctors said would probably never go away.

Sure, some days were better than others, and Hunter tried to keep his thoughts on the positive.

I'm still alive.

I have somewhere to live.

I got an honorable discharge from the Marines.

"Have you been to Hawthorne Harbor?" his driver asked, breaking into Hunter's thoughts.

"Yes," he said without looking away from the ocean. It was beautiful, and he hadn't realized how much he'd missed the sight of it, the smell of it, the constant way it drove toward the shore.

He finally tore his eyes from the water and looked out the windshield. "I grew up there, actually."

"Oh, is your family still here?" The driver was asking to be conversational, Hunter knew. People everywhere seemed to be extra kind to him, and he knew it was because of the uniform he wore and the cane he used. Otherwise, they probably wouldn't even look his direction.

His anxiety tripled when he thought about how his great aunt would receive him, but he pushed it back. After all, Hunter had a ton of experience in burying emotions and getting the job done. And that was what he needed to do in Hawthorne Harbor.

"No," he said. "Well, sort of. My parents moved when I joined the Marines. But there are plenty of Magleby's still in Hawthorne Harbor." Too many, actually, but Hunter kept that info under his tongue. He was looking forward to seeing Aunt Mabel, and she'd told him that Lauren lived just down the hill from the Mansion.

In fact, it would be Lauren who'd fixed up the house where he'd be living, and he had a gift for her in his backpack.

The driver stopped talking then, and Hunter leaned back into the seat behind him, almost hoping time would slow enough to stop. Then he wouldn't have to return to a town that had forgotten him. He wouldn't have to face the past he'd left behind. He wouldn't have to try to figure out who he was now that he wasn't a soldier.

A sigh gathered in his chest, but he kept it contained. Another skill he'd picked up from the numerous meetings he'd endured over the years. He could keep his face completely passive for long periods of time too, and he never, *ever* let his emotions show if he didn't want them to.

He felt like he'd been living behind a slab of stone since the accident that had stolen his mobility from him. Stolen his career.

You're still alive, he started mentally reciting again. You have a good place to live. Family nearby to help. Money coming in.

The road curved, and the ocean moved behind them. The outskirts of town appeared, and Hunter steeled himself to step back in time.

The driver took him right to the house on the northwest side of town, just down the bluff. He jumped out of the car to get Hunter's bags, and Hunter took his time getting out of the backseat and positioning his cane to help balance himself.

"There he is." Lauren came down the front steps, a smile on her face. She didn't even look at his leg or the angry pink scar clawing up from underneath his collar. Her long, dark hair bounced along her shoulders, and a man Hunter didn't recognize followed her. He took Lauren's hand as they approached, and Hunter's wariness returned. He hadn't realized he'd have a whole welcoming committee.

Lauren let go of her boyfriend's hand and embraced Hunter. "You look great."

Ah, so his cousin was a liar now. Hunter smiled anyway. "Thanks. How long have you been back in town?" Her family had left like his, and it was almost an unwritten rules that Magleby's didn't live anywhere but Hawthorne Harbor.

"About seven years," she said. "This is Trent Baker, my husband."

"Oh, congrats," Hunter said, leaning all of his weight on his left leg so he could extend his right hand to Trent.

"Nice to meet you," Trent said, a smile on his face that disappeared quickly.

"Are you Army?" he asked Trent.

"No." Trent shook his head. "I used to be a cop, but now I train dogs to be police animals."

"Ah." So he was in a similar field of work as Hunter. He could always spot those who had some sort of experience dealing with difficult situations, and cops made great soldiers.

"So your place is properly aired out and ready for you," Lauren said, stepping toward the front porch, where the driver had set Hunter's bags. "Trent and I and Porter live just down the road. Aunt Mabel is bringing her apple twist bread by later."

"She doesn't have to do that," Hunter said, looking at the eight steps that led up to the house. The thought of climbing up and down these every day made his muscles tighten and his brain to tell him to find somewhere else to live.

"I know," Lauren said. "But she insisted, and you know how Aunt Mabel can be."

"Pushy?" Hunter said, which caused both Trent and Lauren to laugh. Neither of them reached to help him, which he appreciated. They also didn't walk slower because of him or wait for him. They just went up the steps and into the house, and when Hunter got there, he found three dogs sitting nicely beside Trent.

"This is our welcome home gift to you," Lauren said, beaming down at the canines.

"A dog?" Hunter asked.

"Not just a dog," Trent said. "A trained service animal. They can do all kinds of things."

Hunter blinked, his first reaction to decline a service animal. He wasn't disabled. He didn't need help. But in the back of his mind and way down deep in his hear, he knew he was disabled and he did need help.

"Like what?" he asked.

Trent exchanged a glance with Lauren that didn't go unnoticed by Hunter. "You balance on the couch and hand me your cane." Trent strode forward and took it from Hunter. He put it on the table behind him and whistled at the dogs. All three of them shifted toward him, and one of them whined.

"Sh," Trent said, and the dog quieted immediately. "So you give him a command to get the cane, and he will." Trent pointed to it and said, "Geronimo, get it."

The big German shepherd took a few steps and put his front paws up on the table. He scrabbled around for a moment, finally getting the cane in his jaws and backing up and dropping back to all fours.

"You tell him to bring it," Trent said.

"Bring it," Hunter barked, and the dog trotted toward him, tilted his head back, and let Hunter take the cane from his hand.

"You can tell him to drop it," Trent said. "He can get almost anything you want him to. Geronimo is the one I'd pick for you." He glanced at the other two dogs. "But Clara is great too, and she really likes to cuddle during down-time. So if you like that...." He let his words die there, and Lauren took over.

"Have her open the door," she said.

"You want to see her do that?" Trent didn't wait for Hunter to answer. He walked to the front door while he talked. "So I'll go out and ring the doorbell. You tell her to answer. Just like that. 'Answer it, Clara,' and she will."

He ducked outside and closed the door behind him. A moment later the doorbell rang. All three dogs turned toward it, and Hunter said, "Answer it, Clara."

The smaller golden retriever trotted over to the door and jumped up. With her front paws on either side of the handle, she used her chin to push it down. As she backed up, the door drifted open to reveal a very proud Trent standing there.

Hunter had no idea what to say or do. He knew the dogs made him happy, and he couldn't help smiling. "They're great, Trent. They must cost a lot of money."

"Loads," Lauren said. "So which one do you want?"

He looked at the German shepherd who'd brought him his cane, and the pretty golden retriever who'd opened the door. The third dog had laid down at Lauren's feet, his tongue hanging out of his mouth.

"I like Clara."

"She's yours," Trent said, stooping to scrub down the pup. "He chose you, you lucky girl. Yes, you're so lucky. He wants you."

She grinned up at him and took his praise and affection, and Hunter decided that being back in Hawthorne Harbor wasn't so bad if he could have that pretty dog at his side—and Lauren and Trent just down the street.

THE NEXT DAY, LAUREN PULLED UP TO THE HOSPITAL, AND Hunter said, "I really can go in myself," after she'd offered to accompany him inside.

"All right." She grinned easily at him. "Text me when you're done. I'm on a job site only a block away, and I'll come get you."

"I can probably get a ride." He unbuckled his seatbelt

and opened the door, the autumn wind practically ripping the door off its hinges.

"Really?" Lauren asked. "With who?" At least she wasn't afraid of offending him.

"I don't know," he mumbled.

"So text me."

"Fine." He slid out of her truck, it being much easier to get to his feet from a taller vehicle. He leaned into his cane and limped into the hospital, still twenty minutes early for his appointment.

Still plenty of time, he coached himself. Lots of sick people in the hospital. Hardly anyone glanced his way. You can walk. You're alive.

He kept up the positive self-talk all the way to the elevator and up to the third floor of the hospital, where the physical therapy unit was located. He was sure they'd put it in the farthest corner of the hospital as some sort of sick joke.

An atrium sat on his right, and the hallway beside that led down to the children's wing. A few people sat on the benches with the plants surrounding them, eating lunch. He watched them for a moment, a smile coursing through his body and crossing his face.

A woman eating with a boy sat in the corner, and Hunter's eyes caught on them. She lifted her head, her dark, wavy hair falling over her shoulders and that oh-so-familiar smile lighting up her face as she laughed.

Alice.

Hunter's breath caught in his lungs, and he choked. Plenty of people around to help with that, but he knew he didn't need physical assistance to breathe.

Of course he'd run into Alice Kopp. Her family was Hawthorne Harbor natives, same as his. And he'd left her here when he'd answered his summons to enter active duty, nine years ago.

His wife.

Well, ex-wife now. That marriage had only lasted seven days before Alice had gotten it annulled. Hunter had been notified first by her and then by the court, and he'd never heard from Alice again.

But that woman was definitely her. He'd know her anywhere, as she'd been the first woman he'd fallen in love with. They'd gotten married spontaneously, sure. Irrationally, even. But Hunter had thought they could make it work.

He'd loved her. She'd loved him. That was enough, wasn't it?

Apparently not, and one of the main reasons he hadn't come back to Hawthorne Harbor before now was sitting twenty feet from him.

Alice wore a pair of pale pink scrubs, which meant she obviously worked here, and the child she was with was probably seven or eight years old. Probably a patient, but Hunter watched as Alice checked her watch, said something to the boy, and leaned over to hug him.

They got up together and started toward him. Hunter

panicked, everything in him telling him to move. Get out of the way. Disappear somehow.

Because Alice was going to see him.

Before he could even get his good leg to take a step, she looked up and right into his eyes. She froze.

He was already cemented in place. Behind him, the elevator dinged, and he thought maybe he could just fall backward and the car doors would swoop closed, concealing him.

The boy took a few more steps before turning back and saying, "Mom?"

Mom, Mom, Mom.

The word echoed endlessly in Hunter's head. So Alice had indeed moved on. Found someone else to marry. Had a kid now.

"Well," a woman said, and Hunter managed to turn to look at her. Alice's mother. She hadn't been terribly supportive of Hunter and Alice's youthful romance, nor their shotgun wedding.

"Westin," Alice said, coming up beside the boy quickly. Her voice rang every bell in Hunter's system, and a fool's hope danced through him that they might have another chance. After all, she'd named her son after his father.

Probably a coincidence, he thought. He couldn't even remember her mother's name at the moment. Or his.

She's married with a kid, he told himself as he tried to find

*something solid to grab onto. And you're a lame war veteran
without a job or a purpose.*

Her eyes widened, and she swallowed, clearly nervous
to be face-to-face with Hunter. He wondered if she felt like
she was seeing a ghost, the way he did.

"Isn't this just one big family reunion?" her mother
asked, her tone slightly acidic.

"Family reunion?" Hunter repeated, looking at the
older woman, who had pure white hair now—something
that didn't exist in his memory.

Karen—he was honestly shocked he remembered
Alice's mother's name—turned to her daughter. "You
didn't tell him? You *promised* me you'd told him."

Alice put her arm protectively around the boy, and
Hunter's synapses were firing like cannons. He put all the
pieces together quickly, always good at puzzles.

Westin had dark eyes—like his.

Westin had his mother's dark hair, but Hunter's sloped
nose and square jaw.

"Westin," Alice said, her voice much higher than it
had just been. "This is your father, Hunter Magleby."

Hunter felt like he was falling. Falling forever, the way
he'd been when his tank had been hit. The world spun,
and he flung his arm out, trying to find something to hold
onto. It hit something soft, and her mother seized his
hand and squeezed it.

"Hunter," Alice said, grounding him, centering him,

the way she always had. "Um, this is your son, Westin." She looked at the child and then back to Hunter. "Westin Hunter Magleby."

SNEAK PEEK! THE DAY HE CAME HOME
CHAPTER TWO

Alice Kopp avoided looking at her mother. Or her son. No, she kept her eyes glued to Hunter Magleby, the ghost of a man she'd refused to let go of despite the gulf she'd placed between them.

She slipped her hand out of his as fury roared into Hunter's expression. She put both hands on her son's shoulders, hoping to use him to steady herself. Everything around her felt like it was rocking back and forth. Shaking. Maybe they were having an earthquake right now.

Or maybe all that trembling and breaking and splitting was just happening inside Alice.

"Say something," she said to Hunter, who just stood there, his weight on his cane and his dark eyes storming in a way she'd never seen before. Hunter experienced emotions deeply, she knew that.

They'd fallen in love in a single summer, and the joy

he could broadcast from his eyes was like beholding heaven.

Unfortunately, his anger and stubborn streak ran just as deeply, as she was being reminded now as she stood in front of him. The silent soldier she'd been thinking about for years. And years.

"Alice," her mother said, finally drawing her attention. Alice didn't want to deal with her mother's wrath and disappointment right now either. Her lunch break was minutes from ending, and then she'd have to get back to work.

Her heart felt like someone had tethered it to a live wire, and electricity was zinging it every few seconds.

She looked into her mother's brown eyes, so much like her own, and back to Hunter. "She needs to take Westin, Hunter."

"Maybe he can take me," Westin said, surprising Alice.

"What?" she asked at the same time her mom said, "No, Westin."

"Why not?" Westin and Hunter asked at the same time, further baffling Alice.

"He's clearly here for an appointment," her mother said, looking at Hunter.

"I could go with him." Westin turned and faced Alice. "Right, Mom?"

Alice looked into her son's eyes, so much like his father's. Her heart constricted, and she didn't want to deny him anything.

"How old are you?" Hunter asked, and Westin spun back to him.

"Eight," Westin said. "I'll be nine in March."

"A few months," Alice said, watching Hunter as he did the math. Would he ask for a paternity test? Couldn't he see himself in his son? Alice certainly could, and sometimes she wondered why she'd never said anything to Hunter about the baby. Then the toddler. The little boy. The child.

Deep down, she knew why. She wanted Hunter Magleby to return to Hawthorne Harbor of his own accord, not because she'd drawn him back against his will. A part of her wanted him to return to town for her, too, not because he had to.

But because he *wanted* to.

However, it didn't take her nursing degree to see that Hunter didn't want to be here.

"I do have an appointment in a couple of minutes," he said, his voice softer than it had been a moment ago. He bent down to look into Westin's face. "And they're long, so you can't really come with me."

"But—"

"But we'll see each other again soon."

"Promise?" Westin asked, and Alice's heart folded itself into a tiny box. She knew what it was like to make a promise to her son and then have to break it. She didn't want him to get hurt by Hunter, and immediate guilt flooded her. *She* was the one who hadn't told him about his son. Hadn't given him the opportunity to be a father for eight, long years.

"Of course," he said, straightening. Pain flashed across his face, and Alice's keen nurse's eyes saw it all. His gaze bored into hers, all that fury and frustration returning in a single heartbeat. "I'll call you." Without another word, he turned and limped down the hall toward the physical therapy unit, somehow an angry stomp in his steps even with his injury.

"Go on, Westin," she said, her voice barely more than a whisper and her eyes refusing to let go of Hunter's broad shoulders and long legs.

"Come on, baby," her mom said, gathering Westin into her body. She also met Alice's eyes, and Alice sure hoped someone would look at her with less than contempt that day. "I can't believe you." She shook her head, curled one arm around her grandson, and guided him to the elevator.

Alice felt like someone had filled her veins with ice water, and she rubbed her hands up and down her arms as if cold. Realizing she was late, she hurried back to her station and signed in.

"Who was the handsome man you were talking to out there?" Sadie Benjamin picked up her soda and took a long drink.

"Do you have one of those for me?" Alice sighed and rubbed her forehead though she still had six hours left in her shift.

Sadie nodded toward a Styrofoam cup with a bright

red straw. Relief spread through Alice, and she reached for the drink.

"Oh, he must be someone special," Sadie said.

Alice almost choked on the cold diet cola, the carbonation burning her throat in all the best ways. She sighed again and looked back the way she'd come, though the atrium was down two hallways and couldn't be seen.

"That was Hunter Magleby."

Sadie wasn't from Hawthorne Harbor, but she'd heard enough stories about Westin's father to know to gasp, eyes wide, and cover her mouth with her hand. "You're kidding? He's back in town? Did you know he was back in town?"

"I did not," Alice said, picking up a chart she needed to read. The letters blurred, and she couldn't focus at all.

"And you told him about Westin?"

"I had to. My mother showed up and started throwing around words like *family reunion*." She took another drink of her soda, hoping the caffeine would jumpstart her brain into thinking properly. She started to move out from behind the desk when Sadie stepped in front of her.

"But you would've told him anyway, right?" Sadie looked down at her, and Alice wished she wasn't always looking up into people's faces. "Right, Alice? I mean, Westin is *his son*."

"I know who Westin is," she said, so exhausted she could drop onto a cot in the dark room and sleep for hours. Well, probably not. Her mind would probably circle and obsess and never let her drift off.

No one understood why she hadn't told Hunter about Westin. Alice wasn't sure she understood it either. But no one understood Hunter the way she did. No one knew him the way she did.

Which is all the more reason why you should've told him, she lectured herself. Because she did know he'd be furious. And he wouldn't call. He'd find out where she lived, and he'd stop by her house. Heck, he'd probably be waiting on her front porch when she got home.

"So now what?" Sadie asked, running her fingers through her wavy, blonde hair.

"He's going to call me," she said. "But I'm going to try to catch him after his physical therapy appointment."

"Physical therapy?"

"He was walking with a cane." Concern ran through her, making her heart skip one beat, then two. He'd been injured in his service overseas—exactly as she'd feared he would. Alice didn't want to get into all of her weaknesses today, so she pushed against the emotions rising through her and squinted at the chart.

"Okay, I'm off to little Teddy's room."

"I was just in there," Angela Harding, another nurse, said as she approached the nurse's station. "I gave him the meds. I'll note it." She plucked the chart from Alice's hands with a smile. She scratched a note onto the chart and handed it back to Alice. "Okay, what did I interrupt?"

"Nothing," Alice said, shooting at glance at Sadie.

"Her ex is back in town. Westin's dad. Has a cane and is going to physical therapy."

Ang blinked a few times as she took in all that information. Alice wanted the floor to open up and swallow her whole. Ang's green eyes seemed to draw secrets right out of Alice.

"So we're going for hot chocolate after work," she said.

"I can't," Alice said immediately, thinking of Hunter out in the cold Washington January, waiting for her and Westin to come home.

"Oh, yes, you can." Ang reached over the counter and picked up her phone. "I'll text your mom right now."

"Ang," Alice warned.

"Come on," Sadie said, looping her arm through Alice's. "Come check on the baby twins with me."

"Oh, that's not fair," Alice said, walking away with Sadie but watching Ang over her shoulder. She loved the twin boys who'd been born premature and had spent the first seven weeks of their life in her wing. She loved holding one or both of them during her graveyard shift as they ate. Loved the baby soft feel of their skin. The baby powder scent of their hair and clothes.

But today, even the twin babies couldn't distract her from the thought of coming face-to-face with Hunter again.

∾

AFTER AN HOUR AT THE HOT CHOCOLATE BAR, AND AFTER she'd asked her mom to keep Westin for a little longer, Alice drove slowly down the dirt road that led to one of the Magleby houses. Specifically, the one Hunter had moved into a couple of days ago.

Her headlights cut through the darkness, and she flexed her fingers on the steering wheel. A pit in her stomach told her this was a very bad idea. Hunter had never liked surprises—at least when he was on the receiving end. He loved giving surprises, and the biggest one of all had come when he'd announced he'd joined the Marines after they'd been dating for a couple of months.

The engine idled while she peered at the house on Forgotten Road. It looked more like a log cabin than a house, but it fit in perfectly with all the trees, bushes, and undeveloped land surrounding it. The Magleby Mansion sat on the bluff above the house, and the family owned all the land surrounding it, including the hills, and several houses on this lane and across the highway.

Alice didn't care about any of those houses. She just cared about this one. And not even the house, but the man inside it.

"Go on," she whispered to herself. She'd made the arrangements with Westin so she could talk to Hunter alone. She'd been right; he hadn't called. Maybe he wasn't as resourceful as he'd once been. He'd matured since they'd met at the Lavender Festival in high school. His shoulders had filled out, and his hair had carried a hint of gray when she'd seen him in the hospital.

His thirty-first birthday had come and gone last fall, so he wasn't that old, but he'd definitely had silver hair. He could hide it if he wanted to—the Hunter she'd known and loved could do anything he wanted. He'd asked around until he'd found someone who would give him her phone number, and he'd kept it in his pocket for weeks before calling her.

So why hadn't he called today?

Horrible, traitorous thoughts about how he didn't want to see Westin paraded through her mind.

Please don't let that be it, she prayed as she got out of the car. Her feet ached after her long shift in the children's ward, but she'd endured worse pain. She climbed the steps and employed every ounce of bravery she possessed to knock on the door.

She leaned close to the wood, trying to hear anything behind it.

"Answer it, Clara," she heard, and her pulse bounced like a basketball. Hunter was home, but she had no idea who Clara was. Alice almost bolted. It was dark. He didn't know her car. She didn't know any Clara's, and she was a Hawthorne Harbor native.

Maybe he'd gotten married while he served in the Marines. Maybe that was why he hadn't called. Why he didn't want Westin in his life.

Scratching sounded against the door, and in the next

moment, it opened. It slowly drifted inward, and she saw a beautiful golden retriever sitting there.

"Come, Clara," Hunter said, and the dog immediately trotted over to where he sat in an armchair next to the fireplace. A beat passed, and then he added, "You might as well come in too. It's cold out there."

Alice felt the sting of his words all the way down in her toes. The only reason he wanted her to come in was to keep out the cold. *Doesn't matter*, she told herself as she entered and closed the door.

"Hello, Hunter. Your dog can open the door?"

He simply looked at her, his fingers stroking his retriever slowly. Alice rubbed her hands together and looked around the house. Definitely more of a cabin, with red and blue checkered curtains above the windows and black bear figurines on the mantel.

"Do you even want to see Westin?" she asked, deciding to get right to the point.

"Of course I do," Hunter said, his voice soft but not concealing the undercurrent of anger there. He rose slowly, balancing himself with the armrests of the chair. He stood at his full height, his gaze filled with lasers. "I can't believe we have a child, and you didn't tell me."

Everything inside Alice quivered. Tears sprang to her eyes. She couldn't speak past the huge lump in her throat.

"I'm so angry with you," he said, his quiet fury worse than if he'd yelled. Hunter said so few things, that what he did vocalize actually meant something.

"I know," she said, the tears in her voice as they splashed her face. "I'm sorry, Hunter. I'm so sorry."

He pressed his right hand against his thigh and stepped first with that leg. In stuttering and yet graceful movement, he limped over to the door, giving her a wide berth. "I'd like to take him to breakfast in the morning."

"That's fine," she said. "I usually work graveyards, and he stays with my parents. I was just on the day shift for today, because I have the weekend off."

Hunter opened the door and held onto it tightly. "Is nine o'clock too early?"

"No," she said, wondering if she'd ever feel normal again now that Hunter was back. If she was being completely honest with herself, she hadn't felt normal since he'd left. Her pregnancy hadn't been particularly easy, and she'd lived with the constant fear that Hunter would never return to Hawthorne Harbor. She wasn't sure if she'd worried more about that or if the fact that he could come back had eaten at her more.

No matter what, the last nine years of Alice's life had been a constant roller coaster for her emotions.

"I'll pick him up then. At your mother's?"

"I have my own place."

He reached into his pocket and withdrew a slip of paper. "Text me the address." He extended the paper to her, and she took it, this conversation clearly over.

She moved to go outside, pausing close to him. Too close. Close enough to smell his cologne and see the flecks of blue in those stormy gray eyes. "I'm really am sorry."

He nodded once, his jaw hard and square. He looked somewhere past her, and Alice didn't know what else to do. She'd imagined the moment she'd tell Hunter about Westin, and it had never happened in the hospital atrium.

He had been angry with her, but he'd forgiven her so quickly. She had whole speeches prepared, but all of those words had fled as soon as she'd seen his face. She certainly couldn't spill all her irrational reasons for why she'd never said anything about Westin.

She stretched up on her toes and swept her lips across his cheek. Horrified at what she'd done—eight years ago and now—she scampered out the door and down the steps, leaving Hunter inside his cabin and wishing her heart didn't still beat with excitement at the mere thought of him. And being in the same space? An exquisite kind of torture she wanted to repeat as soon as possible.

BOOKS IN THE HAWTHORNE HARBOR ROMANCE SERIES

The Day He Drove By (Hawthorne Harbor Second Chance Romance, Book 1): A widowed florist, her ten-year-old daughter, and the paramedic who delivered the girl a decade earlier...

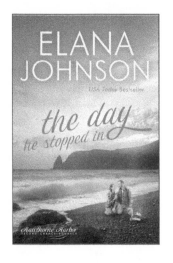

The Day He Stopped In (Hawthorne Harbor Second Chance Romance, Book 2): Janey Germaine is tired of entertaining tourists in Olympic National Park all day and trying to keep her twelve-year-old son occupied at night. When longtime friend and the Chief of Police, Adam Herrin, offers to take the boy on a ride-along one fall evening, Janey starts to see him in a different light. Do they have the courage to take their relationship out of the friend zone?

The Day He Said Hello (Hawthorne Harbor Second Chance Romance, Book 3): Bennett Patterson is content with his boring firefighting job and his big great dane...until he comes face-toface with his high school girlfriend, Jennie Zimmerman, who swore she'd never return to Hawthorne Harbor. Can they rekindle their old flame? Or will their opposite personalities keep them apart?

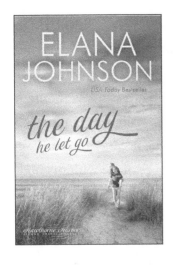

The Day He Let Go (Hawthorne Harbor Second Chance Romance, Book 4): Trent Baker is ready for another relationship, and he's hopeful he can find someone who wants him and to be a mother to his son. Lauren Michaels runs her own general contract company, and she's never thought she has a maternal bone in her body. But when she gets a second chance with the handsome K9 cop who blew her off when she first came to town, she can't say no... Can Trent and Lauren make their differences into strengths and build a family?

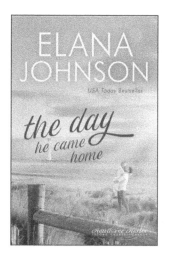

The Day He Came Home (Hawthorne Harbor Second Chance Romance, Book 5): A wounded Marine returns to Hawthorne Harbor years after the woman he was married to for exactly one week before she got an annulment...and then a baby nine months later. Can Hunter and Alice make a family out of past heartache?

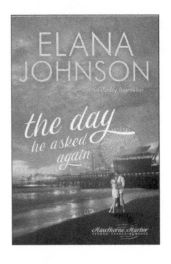

The Day He Asked Again (Hawthorne Harbor Second Chance Romance, Book 6): A Coast Guard captain would rather spend his time on the sea...unless he's with the woman he's been crushing on for months. Can Brooklynn and Dave make their second chance stick?

BOOKS IN THE GETAWAY BAY BILLIONAIRE ROMANCE SERIES

The Billionaire's Enemy (Book 1): A local island B&B owner hates the swanky high-rise hotel down the beach...but not the billionaire who owns it. Can she deal with strange summer weather, tourists, and falling in love?

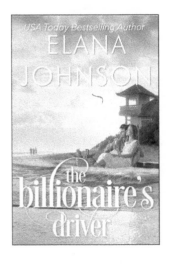

The Billionaire's Driver (Book 2): A car service owner who's been driving the billionaire pineapple plantation owner for years finally gives him a birthday gift that opens his eyes to see her, the woman who's literally been right in front of him all this time. Can he open his heart to the possibility of true love?

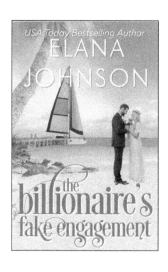

The Billionaire's Fake Engagement (Book 3): A former poker player turned beach bum billionaire needs a date to a hospital gala, so he asks the beach yoga instructor his dog can't seem to stay away from. At the event, they get "engaged" to deter her former boyfriend from pursuing her. Can he move his fake fiancée into a real relationship?

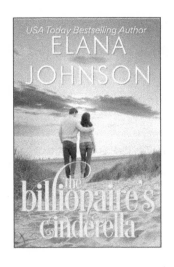

The Billionaire's Cinderella (Book 4): The owner of a beach-side drink stand has taken more bad advice from rich men than humanly possible, which requires her to take a second job cleaning the home of a billionaire and global diamond mine owner. Can she put aside her preconceptions about rich men and make a relationship with him work?

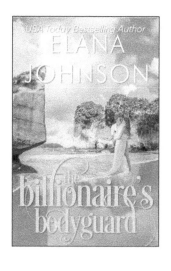

The Billionaire's Bodyguard (Book 5): Women can be rich too...and this female billionaire can usually take care of herself just fine, thank you very much. But she has no defense against her past...or the gorgeous man she hires to protect her from it. He's her bodyguard, not her boyfriend. Will she be able to keep those two B-words separate or will she take her second chance to get her tropical happily-ever-after?

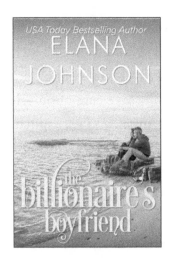

The Billionaire's Boyfriend (Book 6): Can a closet organizer fit herself into a single father's hectic life? Or will this female billionaire choose work over love...again?

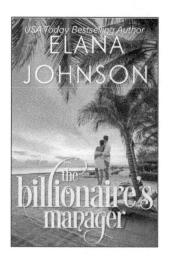

The Billionaire's Manager (Book 7): A billionaire who has a love affair with his job, his new bank manager, and how they bravely navigate the island of Getaway Bay...and their own ideas about each other.

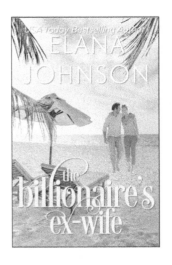

The Billionaire's Ex-Wife (Book 8): A silver fox, a dating app, and the mistaken identity that brings this billionaire faceto-face with his ex-wife...

BOOKS IN THE BRIDES & BEACHES ROMANCE SERIES

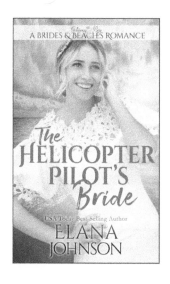

The Helicopter Pilot's Bride (Book 1): Charlotte Madsen's whole world came crashing down six months ago with the words, "I met someone else." Her marriage of eleven years dissolved, and she left one island on the east coast for the island of Getaway Bay. She was not expecting a tall, handsome man to be flat on his back under the kitchen sink when she arrives at the supposedly abandoned house. But former Air Force pilot, Dawson Dane, has a charming devil-may-care personality, and Charlotte could use some happiness in her life.

Can Charlotte navigate the healing process to find love again?

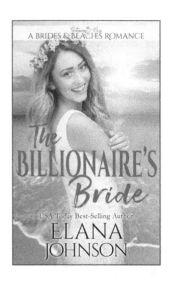

The Billionaire's Bride (Book 2): Two best friends, their hasty agreement, and the fake engagement that has the island of Getaway Bay in a tailspin...

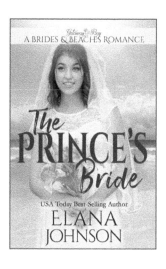

The Prince's Bride (Book 3): She's a synchronized swimmer looking to make some extra cash. He's a prince in hiding. When they meet in the "empty" mansion she's supposed to be housesitting, sparks fly. Can Noah and Zara stop arguing long enough to realize their feelings for each other might be romantic?

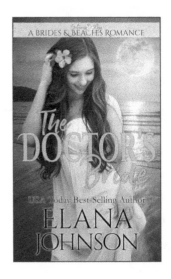

The Doctor's Bride (Book 4): A doctor, a wedding planner, and a flat tire... Can Shannon and Jeremiah make a love connection when they work next door to each other?

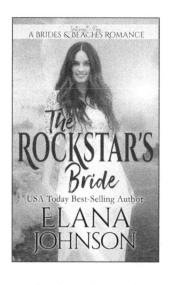

The Rockstar's Bride (Book 5): Riley finds a watch and contacts the owner, only to learn he's the lead singer and guitarist for a hugely popular band. Evan is only on the island of Getaway Bay for a friend's wedding, but he's intrigued by the gorgeous woman who returns his watch. Can they make a relationship work when they're from two different worlds?

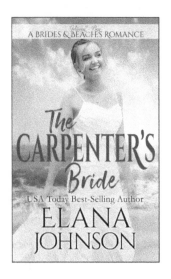

The Carpenter's Bride (Book 6): A wedding planner and the carpenter who's lost his wife... Can Lisa and Cal navigate the mishaps of a relationship in order to find themselves standing at the altar?

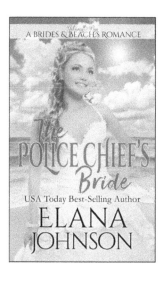

The Police Chief's Bride (Book 7): The Chief of Police and a woman with a restraining order against her... Can Wyatt and Deirdre try for their second chance at love? Or will their pasts keep them apart forever?

BOOKS IN THE STRANDED IN GETAWAY BAY ROMANCE SERIES

Love and Landslides (Book 1): A freak storm has her sliding down the mountain...right into the arms of her ex. As Eden and Holden spend time out in the wilds of Hawaii trying to survive, their old flame is rekindled. But with secrets and old feelings in the way, will Holden be able to take all the broken pieces of his life and put them back together in a way that makes sense? Or will he lose his heart and the reputation of his company because of a single landslide?

Kisses and Killer Whales (Book 2): Friends who ditch her. A pod of killer whales. A limping cruise ship. All reasons Iris finds herself stranded on an deserted island with the handsome Navy SEAL...

Storms and Sentiments (Book 3): He can throw a precision pass, but he's dead in the water in matters of the heart...

Crushes and Cowboys (Book 4): Tired of the dating scene, a cowboy billionaire puts up an Internet ad to find a woman to come out to a deserted island with him to see if they can make a love connection...

BOOKS IN THE CARTER'S COVE ROMANCE SERIES

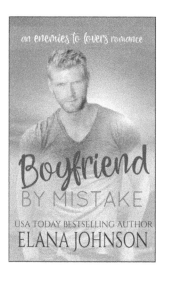

Boyfriend by Mistake (Book 1): She owns The Heartwood Inn. He needs the land the inn sits on to impress his boss. Neither one of them will give an inch. But will they give each other their hearts?

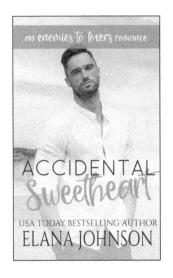

Accidental Sweetheart (Book 2): She's excited to have a neighbor across the hall. He's got secrets he can never tell her. Will Olympia find a way to leave her past where it belongs so she can have a future with Chet?

Bodyguard not Boyfriend (Book 3): She's got a stalker. He's got a loud bark. Can Sheryl tame her bodyguard into a boyfriend?

Not Her Real Fiancé (Book 4):
He needs a reason not to go out with a journalist. She'd like a guaranteed date for the summer. They don't get along, so keeping Brad in the not-her-real-fiancé category should be easy for Celeste. Totally easy.

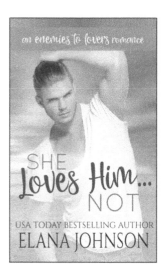

She Loves Him...Not (Book 5): They've been out before, and now they work in the same kitchen at The Heartwood Inn. Gwen isn't interested in getting anything filleted but fish, because Teagan's broken her heart before... Can Teagan and Gwen manage their professional relationship without letting feelings get in the way?

ABOUT ELANA

Elana Johnson is the USA Today bestselling author of dozens of clean and wholesome contemporary romance novels. She lives in Utah, where she mothers two fur babies, taxis her daughter to theater several times a week, and eats a lot of Ferrero Rocher while writing. Find her on her website at elanajohnson.com.

CPSIA information can be obtained
at www.ICGtesting.com
Printed in the USA
FSHW022003130122
87654FS

9 781953 506078